"Why did you leave so quickly, Cass?"

Michael's smile seemed edged in sadness.

She shivered at the question, the memories. "I was sent away because of you, Michael," she whispered, trying to avoid the searching blue of his eyes.

"Because of me? Why?"

"Because no one knew you. Because I wasn't supposed to see you. They thought I made you up, that my imagination was working overtime."

"I'm sorry, Cass, I didn't know." Michael's words were soft and round and full of care. The way they'd echoed in her dreams.

"Is that all you can say?" She faced him squarely, blinking away tears. "Everybody knows everybody around here, isn't that so, Michael? So why didn't anyone know *you*?"

Dear Reader,

Happy Valentine's Day! Love is in the air...and between every page of a Silhouette Romance novel. Treat yourself to six new stories guaranteed to remind you what Valentine's Day is all about....

In Liz Ireland's *The Birds and the Bees*, Kyle Weston could truly be a FABULOUS FATHER. That's why young Maggie Moore would do *anything* to reunite him with his past secret love—her mother, Mary.

You'll find romance and adventure in Joleen Daniels's latest book, *Jilted!* Kidnapped at the altar, Jenny Landon is forced to choose between the man she truly loves—and the man she *must* marry.

The legacy of SMYTHESHIRE, MASSACHUSETTS continues in Elizabeth August's *The Seeker*.

Don't miss the battle of wills when a fast-talking lawyer tries to woo a sweet-tongued rancher back to civilization in Stella Bagwell's *Corporate Cowgirl*. Jodi O'Donnell takes us back to the small-town setting of her first novel in *The Farmer Takes a Wife*. And you'll be SPELLBOUND by Pat Montana's handsome—and magical—hero in this talented author's first novel, *One Unbelievable Man*.

Happy reading!

Anne Canadeo
Senior Editor

Please address questions and book requests to:
Reader Service
U.S.: P.O. Box 1325, Buffalo, NY 14269
Canadian: P.O. Box 1050, Niagara Falls, Ont. L2E 7G7

ONE UNBELIEVABLE MAN
Pat Montana

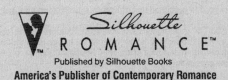

Silhouette

ROMANCE™

Published by Silhouette Books

America's Publisher of Contemporary Romance

To Carole, who started me writing again,
and Morgan, who wouldn't let me give up.
Thanks for believing in me.

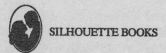 SILHOUETTE BOOKS

ISBN 0-373-08993-7

ONE UNBELIEVABLE MAN

Copyright © 1994 by Patricia A. McCandless

Printed in U.S.A.

PAT MONTANA

grew up in Colorado, but now lives in the Midwest. So far she's been a wife, mother of four adopted daughters and a grandmother. She's also been a soda jerk, secretary, teacher, counselor, artist—and an author. She considers life an adventure and plans to live to be at least one hundred because she has so many things to do.

Some of the goals Pat has set for herself include being a volunteer rocker for disadvantaged babies and teaching in the literacy program. She wants to learn to weave and to throw pots on a wheel, not to mention learn French, see a play at the Parthenon in Greece and sing in a quartet. Above all, she wants to write more romances.

For a wife till death,
I am willing to take ye;
But och I waste my breath
The Devil himself can't wake ye.
'Tis just beginning to rain,
So I'll get under cover;
I'll come to morrow again
And be your constant lover.

—from "Barney Brallaghan's Courtship,"
a comic Irish song by T. Hudson

Chapter One

"My name is Cathleen O'Neil Kohlmann!"

Cassie surveyed the clearing, checking for movement near the broad trunks of the chestnut trees, scanning the shade under the gorse hedge that surrounded the area. She even looked behind the camel-shaped pile of rocks near the center.

"Ooo-kay. If this is an Irish fairy ring, where are all you leprechauns?" she demanded, her bad temper of the last weeks resurfacing.

Reaching to tuck wisps of hair behind an ear, she touched the red bandanna tied around her forehead and remembered her father's words. A seventeen-year-old shouldn't dress like a hippy, he insisted.

Her father? Her jailer! And he wasn't about to let her go back home to St. Louis, so she might as well try to call the leprechauns again. What else was there to do in this Irish wasteland?

"My name is Cathleen O'Neil Kohlmann. Daughter of Molly O'Neil," she added, in case being half-Irish might persuade a response.

"And my name is Michael Padraig Brendan O'Shea." A young man stepped from behind the broadest tree trunk, his thumbs hooked into the pockets of his brown tweed pants. His face softened into lines of humor that made his blue eyes dance.

Cassie swayed back against the rocks and tried to catch her breath. Unbelievable! The legend was true. She'd called out one of the *Daoine Sidh!*

His smile shifted to a look of concern. Pulling a handkerchief from his back pocket, he strode over to her. "Are you ill, Cathleen O'Neil Kohlmann? Shall I go for water?" His words came round and soft, his voice gentle.

She'd never thought a brogue could be so...sexy. "Who are you?" she whispered.

"Michael O'Shea. I was passing by and heard you speaking. No one ever comes to the *rath,* you know. Many Irish believe the fairies live here." The twinkle returned to his deep blue eyes. "Are you a fairy, Cathleen?"

Her face warmed at his teasing. "No, but I thought for a minute you were. But of course those are only legends." She hoped she sounded mature.

"Well now, some of the truest things I know come from stories, Cathleen."

Cassie studied him. The teasing had gone out of his eyes, replaced by curiosity. He looked older than she was, probably mid-twenties, and he wasn't cute exactly, not drop-dead gorgeous, but nice. Handsome. She liked his face, especially when he smiled. For the first time, she was glad to be in Ireland.

"Everyone calls me Cassie except my uncle. And my father," she added with heat.

"Cassie, then. You're the niece of Kevin Malone."

"You know my uncle?" She was glad Michael wasn't a stranger.

"Your uncle talks about you at the stud farm—the little girl of his brother-in-law, come to visit from America."

"Little girl?" she said, a note of indignation in her tone.

Michael grinned down at her. "He changed to 'young lass' after you arrived, but he missed the mark there, too. I didn't expect anyone so pretty—nor with hair so red."

Warmth rose again to her cheeks, and her huff dissolved in confusion. If only she were older.

"Would you care to walk with me to the stud farm, Cassie? To see the horses? 'Tis a fine soft day."

"A fine soft day," the same words Uncle Kevin had used when she'd complained that morning about the gray outside her bedroom window. Now, as she followed Michael through the opening in the hedge, she found that what she'd pronounced dreary and depressing had somehow changed to a gentle misty scene.

She slipped the bandanna off, shaking her curls loose, and stuffed the scarf into her pocket. Her father said she looked older without it. Why was it his logic always won?

Ahead, a bird fluttered up from the grass. Michael stopped. "Look, Cassie, a lark." He counted as more birds followed. "Seven, Cassie, *'Seven for a secret never to be told.'* That's from one of those stories you rejected."

"I wasn't rejecting them, really. I like the stories." If only he knew how she loved make-believe. Her father said she'd learned it from her mother, that they both believed far too easily. He also said that pretending would only get her into trouble.

"The story says the birds tell the future. I think there's a secret in our future, Cassie."

His eyes were so blue, his smile so full of laughter. A gust of wind caught her hair and swept it forward. She let it hide the blush that heated her face.

"Look, Cassie." He pointed to the horizon. The sky had darkened with a storm, and windblown water sketched silver lines from the clouds.

"Storms come in like that from the west, but they usually run out of mischief before they get here. It's rare that we feel one all the way in County Kildare."

The clouds raced overhead, and the wind pressed against their bodies. "I think we'd best head for cover, Cassie. Such weather can knock the top off your head."

She could feel the moisture now, smell it in the air. He held her hand and pulled her along, leaning into the wind.

"It's too far to your uncle's house," he shouted. "We'll go to Glinbrendan. We'll have to run if we're to keep dry."

But they were already too late. Drops of water slanted through the air, splattering their clothes with giant polka dots, making Cassie laugh for the first time in weeks. She felt wonderful, as if she could fly. She tried to shout, but a gust of wind snatched the breath from her mouth.

For a moment, she wondered if she should be afraid. Maybe they'd be caught in a flash flood. Maybe they'd be struck by lightning. "Michael?" She could hardly see him. The wind drove the rain in a diagonal wall, all but blocking him from her view.

He stopped, shielding her from the wind's force with his body. Holding her by the shoulders, he peered down at her. "Are you all right, Cassie? We haven't far to go. Hold tight and follow me." His fingers touched her cheek to brush away skeins of wet hair, a gesture so gentle she shivered.

"Don't be afraid, Cassie. I won't let you drown." He plunged forward, helping her struggle against the driving rain. At last the ground sloped downward, quelling the wind, leaving only the drenching torrent emptying on their heads. Ahead she could make out a white cottage with sheets of water cascading from its thatched roof.

"Hello. *Dia duit,*" he called. The door opened a crack, shouts rang from inside and arms reached out to them. A crowd of young people drew them into a spacious room.

"Are you half-drowned now?"

"Mind you, that's a dirty wind today."

"Likely to give you a dose of pneumonia, and no charge."

A dark-haired girl led Cassie to a chair while another patted her hair with a towel and a third wrapped a blanket tightly around her shoulders.

Cassie looked about in wonder. People! A whole gang of kids who could be her friends, who could make her summer in Ireland fun. In the midst of the uproar, she located Michael seated on a stool enveloped in a blanket. He watched her, lines of amusement curving his mouth.

Her heartbeat somersaulted. Friends. Fun. Michael.

"Cassie," he said, "these are my brothers and sisters." The hubbub subsided as he pointed around the room. "Sheila, Colleen, Liam, Penelope, Sean, Paddy... Fiona and Finn are twins, and this is Katrine." He completed the circle with a proud smile.

Cassie guessed their ages ranged from Michael's mid-twenties to several who looked her age all the way down to the toddler, Paddy, who climbed into her lap.

The bustle quieted when an older woman stepped forward. She had the same blue eyes as Michael, the same black hair except that hers was streaked with silver and drawn back to a twist at her neck.

"Nach 'eil thu faur?" she said, her softly-lined face a mixture of warmth and concern.

"She asked if you're not cold," Michael said. He stood and put his arm around the woman's shoulder. "This naughty woman, who speaks English perfectly well, is our mother, Pegeen O'Shea. Pegeen, this is Cathleen O'Neil Kohlmann."

Cassie suddenly grew dizzy. She knew she should stand and thank Pegeen for her hospitality, but she was afraid if she did, she might faint. Her mother had told her about Pegeen O'Shea. Pegeen was one of the *Daoine Sidh*.

"Michael," Pegeen spoke sharply. "Bring her to the girls' bedroom. Can you not see she's ill? Dragging this tiny lass about in that storm, you ought to be ashamed of yourself. Penelope, the kettle's on the boil. Bring a cup of tea. Sean, get the whisky from your father's cupboard and pour out a good drop."

Michael swept Cassie from the chair, lifting her until she nestled against the wet shirt covering his broad chest. Shocked, she looked up to find his face just inches above her own, his deep blue eyes searching hers with grave concern. Quickly she looked down, her gaze falling to the small mole at the corner of his mouth.

Did fairy folk have moles? she wondered. She had to stop herself from reaching to touch the tiny mark. The impulse made her tremble.

He carried her into the next room and laid her on a bed. With gentle fingers, he brushed wet tendrils of hair from her face before stepping back to let the women take over.

Pegeen helped her drink from a steaming cup that smelled of spice and whiskey. The liquid was hot and tangy.

Imaginary tea wouldn't burn her lips, she tried to reassure herself. Imaginary people wouldn't sleep on beds of down. An imaginary man wouldn't leave her skin tingling from his touch.

"There now, her color's coming back. Out with you lads. Michael, you, too." Pegeen shooed them away and followed close behind. "Girls, get her out of those wet things and into something dry. Fiona, she looks about your size. I'll put her clothes on the hearth to dry. Michael, the fire."

Cassie's tongue refused to work as she watched Michael's sisters. Fiona fetched clothes from a cupboard while two older girls helped Cassie undress and two younger ones collected her things and handed them out to Pegeen.

They slipped a soft blue dress over her head, then toweled her hair again, whispering about its golden-red color.

"Where have you come from, Cathleen?" Sheila asked.

"From America," Cassie managed to say.

The girls sang a chorus of exclamations.

"Why did you come to Ireland?" Colleen asked.

"To visit my aunt and uncle…but really, I'm here for punishment." The words tumbled out before she could stop. She'd had no close friends to confide in for almost a month.

Little by little, they coaxed the story from her, stopping her with questions about things they didn't understand. Things such as a junior prank, and a three-story suburban high school. And especially the cow.

"A cow?" Fiona exclaimed. The other girls giggled.

"It's true," Cassie insisted, her capacity for speech having fully returned. "The boys borrowed a cow from somebody's farm. They told me all I had to do was lead it to the third floor, and they'd bring it back down. Only it turned out that cows won't walk *down* stairs."

When they'd stopped laughing, she had to explain a crane, as it related to a balky cow.

"The principal called my father, and my father was so mad, he sent me here." Her mother wouldn't have sent her away. If her mother were still alive, she would have understood.

A resounding knock interrupted. "If Cassie's dressed, you should bring her out by the fire," Michael commanded.

"We can't find a thing to put on her, Michael," Colleen called back. "She'll have to stay in here till her clothes are dry." The girls giggled. "Or else you boys will have to leave so we can bring her out in a blanket."

"You'd best wrap her well then, for I'm coming to get her. She should be by the fire." Michael sounded cranky.

"Quick, Cathleen." Fiona waved Cassie into a cupboard.

"All right, where is she? What have you done with her?" Michael demanded, pushing into the room.

"She's gone, Michael," Colleen teased. "She was one of the *Daoine Sidh,* you know, and since we don't believe in such fancies, she just disappeared."

"That's enough, Colleen. She should be warming by the fire, so she'd better reappear right away." He sounded in no mood to deal with sisters. Not wanting to cause a family feud, Cassie stepped from the cupboard.

"Look, Michael, now that you're here, we can see her again," Colleen said. "You must be a true believer." She ruffled his hair, then dodged his swat.

Scowling, Michael led Cassie into the big room where he settled her into a rocking chair near the hearth and tucked a blanket around her knees. Sitting in the opposite chair, he surveyed her, his frown slowly dissolving.

Cassie leaned back and stretched her sock-covered feet toward the fire, avoiding Michael's eyes. All this attention made her uneasy. She'd set out this morning to the fairy ring on a whim, to relieve her boredom—and her loneliness. Now things had become serious.

Pegeen bent to feel Cassie's forehead. "Your color is better, Cathleen. How are you feeling?"

"I feel much better, Mrs. O'Shea." Pegeen's fingers on her face felt real, though less tender than Michael's.

"You must call me Pegeen, as everyone does."

"Pegeen." Cassie tested the name, then took a deep breath. "Michael's sisters were teasing him about...I mean, I'd like to ask about the *Daoine Sidh*." A glance passed between Michael and Pegeen, but Cassie plunged on. "I was very young when my mother told me the legend and I don't remember—"

"We'd be happy to share that Irish lore with you, Cathleen. Michael, tell her the legend of the Good People."

Michael looked uncomfortable, but he hesitated only a second. Everyone settled on the floor to listen.

"Many years ago, Cassie, Ireland was ruled by the *Tuatha de Dannan*. They were good people, and they loved this land, but they were conquered by the Milesians who *banished* them from Ireland." He paused while his audience gasped. They'd obviously heard the story many times.

"They couldn't bear the thought of leaving Ireland," he continued, "so they evolved into the *Daoine Sidh*, people who couldn't be driven away, because they couldn't be seen."

Cassie laughed. "What a way to solve their problem."

"Aye, the Good People were clever, Cassie. They were builders and poets and musicians. And they bred horses the likes of none others in the world—fleet as the wind, made of fire and flame, shod in silver with bridles of gold."

"Enough about horses, Michael," Fiona interrupted from her spot next to Finn at Cassie's feet. "Cathleen wants to hear about people."

"Ah, yes. The Good People were skilled in magic. They could become whatever they wished, change whenever they chose. They're full of mischief, too. Some never leave off playing tricks." Michael gave Colleen's hair a tug.

"Uncle Kevin said that *some* people can see them." Again Cassie felt more than saw a reaction in the O'Sheas.

"In Glinbrendan 'tis said the *Daoine Sidh* can be seen, but only when they are *with* someone who truly believes in them." Quiet followed Michael's words.

"Don't forget to tell her," Fiona added dreamily, "if a mortal truly loves one of the Good People, he will become visible everywhere—forever. He will become a man again."

"There are many versions of the legand, Cathleen." Pegeen spoke in a tone that was at once kind but firm.

Sensing the storytelling was coming to a close, Cassie turned to Pegeen. "My uncle said one of the Good People is known by name in County Kildare. He said the name is . . . Pegeen O'Shea."

"I've heard that, too, and I'm honored," Pegeen said. "But surely you understand 'tis a common name in Ireland."

"I . . . never thought of that." Cassie's face grew hot. She hoped she hadn't been rude.

She peeked at Michael, expecting disapproval, but his smile came easily, his gaze soft on her face. Relieved, she saw that the others looked more relaxed, too.

"Cathleen, you seem much better," Pegeen said, "And so is the weather." Sunshine streamed through the window. From the mantel, Pegeen removed Cassie's sweatshirt and jeans and patted them for dampness. "Your clothes are dry. It's getting late, and your family will be worrying."

When Cassie returned from changing, everyone had gathered to say goodbye, everyone except Michael.

"Céad mile fáilte," said Pegeen. "You will always have one hundred thousand welcomes in our home, Cathleen O'Neil Kohlmann. Perhaps the next time you come, you'll meet Padraig O'Shea who is husband and father in this house. He is probably drying out at someone else's fire right now."

Cassie moved from one O'Shea to the next, returning the hugs they offered, trying not to search for Michael. Fiona whispered, "I hope you'll come back," and when Cassie knelt to hug Paddy, he gave her a wet kiss.

At the door, Pegeen placed firm hands on Cassie's shoulders. "You're a lovely young lass, Cathleen, with more than a bit of spunk. I like that. Michael will take you to your aunt and uncle's, and you must come back to Glinbrendan soon."

Horse's hooves pounded nearby, drawing them outside to discover Michael astride a giant black stallion.

Cassie stared up at him. She'd never ridden with another rider nor on such a huge horse, and she'd certainly never ridden bareback. But she had little time to contemplate her situation, for on the count of three, Michael swung her up and settled her behind him. "Put your arms around my waist, Cassie."

She tried to keep from brushing him, but the animal leaped forward making her clutch Michael's hard middle. She could smell the scent of his warm skin through the broad weave of his shirt, could feel his muscles tighten and stretch beneath her breasts pressed so tightly against him. Fear gave way to a rush of heat, to excitement that set her heart racing like the horse's hooves all the way across the pastures of Glinbreandan.

When they reached her uncle's house, Michael pulled the horse to a stop and helped her slide to the ground.

"You're coming in, aren't you?" she managed to ask, still finding it hard to breathe. She didn't want him to go. Not until she found out when she'd see him again.

He hesitated, taking time to study the house. Finally, he dismounted with a leap.

Cassie led him into the cottage, her heartbeat barely easing. "Aunt Brigid?" she called, hurrying to the kitchen. On the table lay a note which she skimmed. "They've gone to look for me. Will you wait, Michael?"

He glanced out at the dimming sky. "Are you feeling all right, Cassie?"

"I'm fine, really. Thank you for bringing me back. And thank you for saving me from drowning."

"The storm was not welcome, Cassie. But you were."

His incredible blue eyes held her as she walked with him back outside. She felt shy again and warm, and strangely happy.

He stopped near the great horse, kicked at a stone, shoved his hands deep into his pockets. "Perhaps I'll see you again, Cassie. I'd like to see you again." He hesitated. "Tomorrow. Yes, tomorrow." Kicking the stone away, he swung up onto his horse and urged the animal into a trot.

His last words had sounded like a promise. "I hope so, Michael," she whispered. She hoped she'd see her new Irish friends, but more than anything, she hoped she'd see Michael. Tomorrow.

Just moments after Michael's departure, a truck turned off the road and slowed to a stop in front of the house. Cassie ran to meet it.

"Cassie, thank God you're safe." Aunt Brigid bustled from the pickup to wrap her niece in a hug. "We were so worried."

"That was some storm, Cathleen." Uncle Kevin hugged her in turn, then held her at arm's length. "But look at you. You're dry as a bone, with rosy cheeks to boot. Where've you been now, lass?"

"Uncle Kevin, I had such a wonderful time. I met your workmate Michael O'Shea, and he took me to Glinbrendan. I met his brothers and sisters, and I think Fiona will be my best friend. And I met Pegeen O'Shea! She's very nice and not a fairy person at all, and neither is—" She saw the look that passed between her aunt and uncle.

Aunt Brigid felt Cassie's forehead. "You'd better come into the house and let me take your temperature."

"I feel fine. What's the matter?" She knew something bad was coming.

"Cathleen . . ." Uncle Kevin sounded as if he were talking to a very small child. "Nowhere nearby is there a place called Glinbrendan. And no one in the whole of County Kildare is called Pegeen O'Shea. And, lass, I have no workmate named Michael O'Shea."

Chapter Two

Ten years later

Cass eased through the thorny branches that threatened to run her nylons, to snag her jade suit and short-
cropped hair. Once inside, she halted at the edge of the
clearing, her pulse pounding.

This had to be the place—the encircling hedge grown
more concealing in the ten years since she'd so unwill-
ingly left, the giant trees casting deceptive shadows, the
odd pile of rocks that had reminded her of a sleeping
camel.

She shivered despite the afternoon's warmth and
clasped herself in a reassuring hug. She shouldn't have
come back.

Squaring her shoulders, she took seven strides into the
clearing, repeating softly, "'Seven for a secret never to
be told.'" She surveyed the shadows, then took a deep
breath.

"My name is Cathleen O'Neil Kohlmann." Even as she said the words, she couldn't believe she was doing this. Ten years ago when her father had shipped her back to St. Louis, she'd vowed never to return to Ireland. Yet here she was, a grown woman, not only back in Ireland but back in a fairy ring trying to call out spirits. Surely she'd lost her mind.

She scanned the clearing again. The urge to leave was strong, and her shoulders tensed with the strain of staying. She'd try one more time. Reluctant to give credence to the stories, she only thought her name. Squinting, she searched the *rath* carefully. As she'd expected, she was alone.

Alone. Memories of her last anguished visit to the fairy ring surfaced despite her efforts to forget them, memories of that morning ten years ago when she'd risen before the sun and run almost the whole distance from her uncle's house. At the *rath,* she'd charged in.

"Michael! Where are you? I need to talk to you."

Catching her breath, she faced the rocks and called out her name. Less confident, she tried again. No one appeared.

She slumped against the rocks, tears stinging her already puffy eyes. What could she do? Her aunt and uncle didn't believe her visit to Glinbrendan, although they hadn't actually accused her of lying. They just thought she was ill.

If only they hadn't told her father. If they hadn't telephoned him in Cork where his American company had transferred him. She'd known how he would react. He'd accused her of making up stories. If she didn't find Michael to confirm what had happened, her father would

send her back to St. Louis—that very afternoon—to live
with her stern, conservative grandparents.

"Michael, where are you?" She could feel the emptiness of the clearing. She was shouting at air and expecting Michael to appear before her eyes.

Maybe she *was* sick. Maybe she'd dreamed him and his
dark blue eyes, his hard muscular body. Maybe she'd
imagined the whole afternoon, cooked up from the stories her mother had told her. Maybe her father would win
again.

Her mother would have believed her. If only she
hadn't...died. Cassie hated the word. Remembering her
mother's stories made the sadness go away. She still
wanted to believe in leprechauns...because her mother
had. She wanted to believe in Michael.

"I'm leaving, Michael," she said to the empty air. "I
came to say goodbye. My father's sending me away."
Only the soft coo-cooing of a dove answered her words.

From her pocket, she pulled out the red bandanna and
laid it on the camel shaped rocks. A tear slid down her
cheek. "Goodbye, Michael...."

She'd never seen him again. And she obviously wasn't
going to see him now. Well, she didn't believe in leprechauns anymore. She brushed moisture from under her
eyes and tucked a few short strands of hair firmly behind an ear.

So, that was that. Aunt Brigid and the rest of the family would be pleased. Her father would have been especially happy. She wished she could have told him before
he died. With a sigh, she turned to leave.

"I'd almost given you up, lass."

She whirled around. "Michael!" Her heartbeat
quickened.

He lounged back against the camel rocks, his legs crossed at the ankle, his arms folded casually across his chest.

"No," she murmured, watching the slow smile she remembered so well pull at the corner of his mouth. "Go away. I don't want to see you."

"Then why did you come here, Cassie? You cannot find a thing except in the place it is."

"Don't talk blarney, Michael O'Shea." She watched him unwind and push away from the rocks, his half smile warming.

Damn him, he wasn't supposed to be here. She wasn't supposed to hyperventilate at the sight of him. She took a deep breath and held it, forcing herself to examine him.

He'd changed. No longer the lean young man who'd carried her across The Curragh on the black stallion, he stood taller, and he'd "filled out just grand," as Uncle Kevin would say. His tweedy work pants and faded shirt covered a body more muscular than she remembered. His curly black hair was shorter, his face honed to strong planes and well-worn lines that told of laughter, frequent and deep. Only his eyes hadn't changed. They were the same unearthly blue. She recalled how he'd watched her, making her skin tingle—as it did now.

She crossed her arms, to hold herself from running away, to keep from moving closer. "I didn't expect to find you here, but I'll say goodbye now since you didn't show up the last time. *Slán agat,* Michael."

"If you're going to be saying goodbye, the least you can do is visit a bit before you go." The melody of his words reminded her of the first time she'd heard his brogue. His voice was richer now, more persuasive.

A patch of red extended from his pocket. "You found my scarf." She stepped forward, reached out, then willed herself to stop.

"Aye, and kept it, hoping you'd be back for it someday."

"Michael, why didn't you come when I called you that morning?" The words spilled forth, colored with the anguish of all her old uncertainties.

"I couldn't hear you all the way to my father's house."

So he heard the same as any mortal. After all these years of doubt, was she finally to accept that he was real?

"I'm sorry about your father's death, Cass."

A shiver rippled through her at his soft sympathy. He'd called her Cass. He no longer regarded her as a girl.

"That's how I knew you'd be coming. I've been waiting for you . . . to tell you this. On weekends when your father came to visit, he was learning to ride. But he was riding alone this time—he never did that, you know—and something must have spooked his horse. His head hit a rock. He went right away." He cleared his throat. "He knew no pain."

Something about his tone made her look more closely, but his feelings were hidden behind those watchful eyes. "Michael, how do you know all this?"

"A death like that is the talk of County Kildare, Cass. With so many good riders here, a fatal fall is rare."

"Of course." Her throat tightened, and she had to turn away. "I hadn't seen him for three years. I don't think he believed even then that I'd . . . grown up."

"He went to see you for Christmas that year," he said, almost as if to himself.

His tone brought her head up. "How do you know these things?"

This time it was he who turned aside. "Your uncle talks about you at the stud farm. He misses you, Cass."

"Michael, my uncle said he didn't know you."

"It's a big place..." He hesitated before continuing. "...and we don't work in the same...areas."

"I find that hard to believe." She didn't try to keep the mistrust from her voice.

"Just as you don't believe in the legends?" His smile seemed almost edged in sadness. "Why did you leave so quickly, Cass?"

She shivered at the questions, the memories. "If you learned so much, Michael, why couldn't you find that out?"

"All I know, Cass, is that one day we met, and the next day you were gone. Your uncle told it about that you'd gone to your grandparents." He seemed to weigh his thoughts, then added softly, "I'd hoped you'd be here all summer."

So had she. His painful reminder stole her voice. "They sent me away because of you, Michael," she whispered. She reached to push a phantom curl behind an ear, avoiding the searching blue of his eyes.

"Because of me? Why?"

"Why?" Her voice rose. "Because no one knew you. Because I wasn't supposed to see you. They thought I made you up, that my imagination was working overtime because I didn't have any friends here." She struggled to keep the tears of adolescent memories from rising. "My father said I was too old for that kind of make-believe, for that *Daoine Sidh* business. He sent me back to reality."

She lowered her head. "My uncle probably never talked about it because he didn't understand. None of them knew what to make of a crazy little carrot-top who claimed she'd seen a...man, and a family and a town they'd never heard of.''

"I'm sorry, Cass, I didn't know." Michael's words were soft and round and full of care. The way they'd echoed in her dreams.

"Is that all you can say?" She faced him squarely, blinking away tears. "Everybody knows everybody around here, isn't that so, Michael? Why didn't they know you?"

"I didn't know you suffered so because of me, Cass. I'm truly sorry." He moved close, reaching a hand to her.

His soothing words thickened his brogue and left her wanting more of his comforting. Wanting him to brush her hair from her face as he once had.

Instead, she took a step backward and let the moment pass. "I don't need your comfort, Michael. What I need is to know that you're real and I'm not crazy. I'm going home tomorrow, and I intend to forget all about you. I have a very real, very uncrazy life in America."

"Aye, Cass, I can tell by just how happy you look...which is about the same as a fox on the run from the hounds."

She raised her hand to protest, and he grasped her wrist. His strong warmth left no question about his reality. His smile denied the dark feelings she thought she'd detected.

"Listen, Cass Kohlmann. You're not crazy. You're much too headstrong for that—and much too pretty." He looked at her clenched fist and grinned. "And I do not think I'd like you to punch me."

"Let go of me, Michael." His touch raised longings she intended to leave in Ireland this time.

His grin deepened, but he dropped her hand.

She hurried to the opening in the hedge. Even as she twisted through, she could hear him talking.

"As for being known, you can ask anyone, Cass. Mick O'Shea is well respected these days in County Kildare. You needn't be ashamed to call him your friend."

He emerged from the hedge and caught her by the arm. Pulling her to him, he held her with strong hands, with unreadable eyes, making it impossible for her to tell which made her tremble. A murmur of protest was all she could manage before he leaned to kiss her, softly, firmly, a kiss that sent shock waves rocking through her.

"Tell me that's not real, Cass," he whispered.

He'd planted the idea but a moment before, and she couldn't stop herself. She swung with the force of feelings too long locked up. The flat of her palm connected sharply with the breadth of his cheek, leaving her hand smarting.

Shock vied with shame while she watched his face redden. She'd never struck a person in her life, yet rubbing her stinging hand she felt a strange, almost obstinate relief. "I'd say that was very real, Michael."

He touched his cheek, surprise and humor dancing in his eyes. Laughter rumbled from him. "There now, headstrong is what I said," he announced between breaths.

"Damn you, Michael." She turned on her heel and strode away. He had her acting like the teenager she'd been.

"Let's go, Cass." He caught up, amusement still coloring his words. "I'm going with you to talk to your aunt and uncle, to put an end to your crazy reputation. Then they'll think you the proper sane woman you want to be." His sympathetic smile softened the bite of his words.

"No."

She stopped. What was she saying? He'd offered to set things straight with her family. Though she'd gone to the *rath* for her own peace of mind, she wanted their respect.

College degree, CPA certification, job as a senior in a major accounting firm, none of her achievements—not even the fact that she was dating her boss, Blake Brockman—could compete with a living, breathing O'Shea to prove her rationality. Michael was a reality her relatives could see. That made him the best proof.

Reluctantly, she called after him. "Michael, you're going the wrong way. My car's down on the road. I'm going to the funeral home in Kildare."

"Then I'll be coming along."

She started to object, then thought better of it. Michael owed her, for all the misgivings her family held, for the painful self-doubt she'd lived with. Only her best friend Jenny had believed in her. Jenny would tell her to keep Michael around until he set things right.

Okay. She'd take him back to the house. Her aunt and uncle could hear his story and shake his very solid, very real hand. Once they accepted that what she'd claimed ten years ago was true, she'd leave that whole unhappy chapter of her life—and Michael O'Shea—behind forever.

Her fingers strayed to her mouth, to the lingering warmth of his lips. Firmly, she tried to brush the kiss away. She was forging a good solid life for herself. She didn't need this Irishman stirring up...complications.

Michael moved around the sleek little car with no top, sliding his hand over the gleaming white paint, breathing in the smell of the leather seats that shone the color of wine.

How he'd loved riding in this carriage with Wil Kohlmann. How he'd hated seeing it stand so empty just two days ago at the stud farm where he'd rushed after hearing of Wil's fall.

"A fine carriage, Cass." A fine thing indeed, just like its driver, he thought, settling into the other seat. He turned to savor another look at her.

He'd waited so long. She was no longer the skittish colt he'd risked befriending ten years ago. Though she was still as small as a leprechaun, she was grown now with the full curves of a woman. And her hair, it had mellowed to a rich chestnut. But she wore it much too short.

"Cass, why did you cut your hair?" She looked like a windblown elf. She should wear it long and loose to fall around her fair face—and over a man's hands.

"Not that it's any of your concern, but it's appropriate for business." She steered the car onto the road.

Careful, Michael, me lad. Questions made her eyes flash, and a kiss made her strike like lightning. He'd best start behaving or he'd lose her again.

She'd come back to the *rath*. She'd wanted to see him. Over the years, he'd all but given up hope, but when he spoke to her there and she'd turned back, he knew she hadn't put him out of her mind, any more than he had her.

Of course her reasons were different—she'd made that clear. He hadn't thought her family would react so strongly. She'd been hurt, and badly, that showed in her face. It made him want to comfort her. Made him risk that long-imagined kiss.

He'd never intended her harm. Quite the opposite, he'd liked her from the first. More than that...she'd fired his imagination as no other lass had. And though she'd seemed very young, that had suited him then. He'd thought they had time. The truly good things took time—Pegeen had told him that often enough.

If only they'd had the whole summer together. When he'd found her scarf there in the clearing, he'd known she was gone. The waiting had begun when he'd realized he missed her in ways a man didn't miss someone who was just a friend.

Pageen had warned him—'twas a danger to step into the world of a believer. He could see that a great deal of harm had resulted from all that he'd dared to share with Cass that day. A tight harness had been placed on this little filly. He just hoped her spirit wasn't broken.

Cass turned the car down a dirt lane, and he caught sight of a small house at the end. Stopping in front, she hurried to the door, and he vaulted out to follow.

"Aunt Brigid, I'm back. I want you to meet someone."

Inside, no one answered. Michael followed Cass to the kitchen where she picked up a slip of paper from the table and read aloud. "Cass, I've gone to a neighbor's. Back in time to start supper."

Michael felt the same disappointment he saw in her face. He wanted to set things right. He wanted to erase the hurt of a young girl, to capture the trust of the woman. He wanted Cass to see him through a woman's eyes.

"Why don't I ride into Kildare with you? We can come here again on the way back." He brushed his fingers through his hair, combing it for the trip into town.

Cass looked up at him guardedly. She was being cautious—he hated to see that in her. Unexpectedly, her delicate features sharpened. Her gray eyes flashed like the sheen of silver, reminding him of the spark he'd seen that day in Glinbrendan, the spark that had struck fire in him.

She'd decided to keep him around until he had his say with her aunt and uncle. She wouldn't say goodbye yet.

Still, he knew it was too soon to relax. He'd have to avoid talk of Pegeen and Glinbrendan. He'd have to be very careful and very gentle, because he really did want to make up for the hurt he'd caused. He really did want to convince Cass he was real.

He had to, if he was going to persuade her to take him with her. To keep him with her—all the way to America.

Outside the Donovan Funeral Home, Cass stepped from the sports car and watched Michael fumble with his door latch. She almost regretted that she'd let him come along. She wanted nothing to divert Mr. Donovan while he completed the final arrangements. More important, she wanted nothing to distract her. Much as she tried to resist it, Michael did distract her.

Once inside, they were greeted by a thin, white-haired man. "Ah, Miss Kohlmann." He reached for her hand, then turned to Michael, peering through his wire-rimmed glasses.

"Mr. Donovan, this is Michael O'Shea, a...friend. He's come to help me finalize the arrangements."

Still holding her hand, Mr. Donovan squinted at Michael. "Michael O'Shea. Name sounds familiar. Can't place it right now, but I will. Know all the people in Country Kildare, buried a good many of 'em, as I should be burying Wil Kohlmann. Like blood kin to your uncle, he was."

"Sure, now, Mr. Donovan—"

"I know," Cass interrupted Michael. "My aunt and uncle loved my father, but I don't want my parents to be buried apart. Please, have you made all the arrangements?"

"Not right to move a body around like he was on vacation," Mr. Donovan muttered, shuffling to a small desk in the corner. "Bad enough that he couldn't have a proper Catholic service. How's a soul to rest in peace?"

His head bobbed up from a drawer. "Ah, here they are. Mr. O'Shea, talk some sense to her." He handed a sheaf of papers to Michael. "Look here," he fussed, tapping his finger on the papers. "The casket will go tomorrow morning. We'll at least send it by hearse, but 'twill be a long ride all the way to Dublin. To Dublin airport—the airport, mind you. He'll be bouncing about in one of them airplanes when he should be resting in the peace of angel wings."

"Mr. Donovan—"

"Not only that," the pacing man added, ignoring Michael, "he'll have to change planes in New York, and it'll be a miracle if he doesn't get lost. The only help I could give was to put him on Aer Lingus to the airport named Kennedy." Mr. Donovan dropped his hands to his sides with a slap. "I tell you, a man should be left to rest in peace."

"Mr. Donovan, Cass wants—"

"Everything's been confirmed, Mr. Donovan?" Cass took the papers from Michael, cutting off his words.

"Aye." Mr. Donovan sighed. "Those are the official documents from the consulate. You can pick up your father in St. Louis day after tomorrow. I'd suggest you put him to rest right away as he'll not be standing the heat too well."

"Oh, dear." She'd been shocked to learn the Irish didn't embalm their dead. She had to get her father home quickly, and Mr. Donovan's arrangements only complicated the trip. But it was too late to alter things now.

"Come along, Miss Kohlmann. You'll be wanting to say goodbye."

"Michael, wait for me here," she called back.

Standing before her father's casket, Cass was amazed, as she had been at the wake yesterday, that he looked so peaceful. He'd always been so serious and stern, qualities that, over the years, had kept them apart. If only she could have known that he'd believed in her before he died.

"Dad, I hope you think I'm doing the right thing." The practical solution—her father had always been practical—would be to bury him right there in Ireland instead of dragging him so many miles. But it just didn't seem right to let logic dictate this time, in such an emotional matter. She stared down at her father a moment longer. "I'll look after you, Dad," she whispered.

When she returned to the reception room, Michael was nowhere to be seen. "Mr. Donovan, where's Michael?"

"I do not know, Miss Kohlmann. I turned my back, and he just disappeared."

Concerned, she hurried to leave. "Thank you for everything, Mr. Donovan."

"Goodbye, Miss Kohlmann. God bless." He stood in the doorway muttering, "Michael O'Shea? Michael O'Shea?"

Cass tried to ignore a tiny shaft of fear. "Michael O'Shea, indeed," she grumbled, hurrying to the side of the building where she'd parked the car. A lot of help Michael had been with Mr. Donovan. And where was he now? Had he decided not to talk to her relatives after all? Or had he really just up and disappeared?

Chapter Three

Cass rounded the corner of the Donovan Funeral home to find Michael tilted halfway back in the passenger seat of the white sports car, studying the sky. Vaguely she acknowledged a flicker of relief.

Michael looked almost as if he belonged in the car. Much more so than her father would have. Tight-fisted Wil Kohlmann buying such a luxury? She had trouble believing that. The sporty convertible suited her father about as well as a tank suited her. He must have bartered for a phenomenal price.

He'd surely have disapproved of how much she was spending to take him home. Doubts about her decision returned, sweeping all other thoughts aside. Leaving her with only an elusive anger . . . that he'd died at all.

"So you didn't disappear," she hurled at Michael.

He leaped out and dashed round the car to open her door. Cass threw herself into the seat. Turning the key until the engine shrieked, she jammed the transmission into gear, sending gravel flying. With a shout, Michael jumped in beside her.

She veered through traffic, grief and anger expanding inside of her like a balloon. The road carried them to the peaceful green pastures of the countryside, but the tightness in her chest didn't ease.

"'Tis difficult to say goodbye to a loved one." Michael's voice was full of sympathy.

Cass knew if he treated her kindly, she might cry. She hadn't cried yet for her father. "A lot of help you were, Michael O'Shea," she accused, almost hoping for a fight, for an excuse to release the sharp hurt that tumbled inside her.

"You didn't need my help, Cass," he soothed. "I left because I only seemed to ruffle Mr. Donovan. He was a nervous old dobbin, and you handled him like an expert."

Her chest unknotted a little. "I thought you'd run out."

"I'm here, aren't I, Cass?" He captured her gaze, his indigo eyes holding hers, an inviting smile tugging the corners of his mouth.

Aftershocks of his earlier kiss rippled through her, a response that lingered, upsetting her even more than her anger. Frowning, she looked back to the road.

"Besides, it's a long walk back to Glinbrendan," he added.

She could hear the grin in his voice. Damn. Blarney came in more forms than words, and Michael knew them all. She'd have to ignore him until he told their story to her aunt and uncle. Then she'd say goodbye for good.

"Sounds like a bit of an adventure you and your father will be having, Cass. Are you sure you'll be all right?"

"Yes, of course. I've traveled a lot. I'll take the first train from Kildare in the morning and monitor his trip all the way. Everything will be fine." If there were problems, she'd deal with them. She was accustomed to handling difficult situations. Blake Brockman had hired her for such talents. Asked her out because he valued them. The thought did little to reassure her.

"Cass, I've been thinking that you'll be needing some help. I'll just come along with you to St. Louis to see that your father doesn't get lost."

"What?" Her heart thudded against her ribs.

"Easy, easy now," he murmured. "It was just an offer."

"Thank you, Michael, but I can take care of my own responsibilities." She was overreacting, she knew, and she couldn't seem to help it. She'd steeled herself to face his charm for as long as it took to clear things up with her family. Beyond that, she wasn't prepared for Michael.

He settled back, whistling what sounded like a jig.

Cass tried to get a grip on herself as they approached the familiar cottage. Pulling the car to a stop, she jumped out. "Let's get this over with. Aunt Brigid, I'm back," she called into the house. "There's someone here to meet you."

The silent rooms were absent of the usual rich smells of cooking at that time of day. Michael followed her into the kitchen where she stood reading another note. Her hand flew to tuck strands of hair behind an ear.

"What is it?"

"Uncle Kevin had to stay at the stables. Aunt Brigid took a meal to him. One of the mares was having trouble foaling and—"

"May I see?" Michael plucked the note from her hand and scanned it quickly, his face suddenly tense with conflict.

"I . . . must go." He returned the paper, frowning.

"Where are you going?" She hurried after him into the small yard. "Michael, you can't just leave. You promised."

He turned to clasp her shoulders. Just as quickly, his mouth closed over hers, his lips claiming her in a kiss so gentle yet so consuming that her anguish stilled and her heart must have surely stopped. His eyes held hers with questions while he slipped her scarf around her neck and tied it loosely. He stood looking down at her, his palm cupping her face, his callused thumb tracing her lips. She was afraid to read what was in his eyes.

Then he was gone, jogging into a close-growing stand of chestnuts and out of sight. Cass stood staring after him, her fingers moving to her tingling mouth.

"Wait! Michael! You . . . can't . . ." She followed, her voice trailing away. Slowing to a stop, she searched for his figure among the trees.

How could she reason when her heart thundered so? The note . . . Aunt Brigid's note. Of course. He was going to the stables—to help with the foaling. She dashed to the car, then stood staring down at it. She didn't know the way to Hugh Finnegan's stables.

She should have known. She should have known better than to accept Michael's offer. All she'd done was reopen painful wounds. Her aunt and uncle didn't need proof anymore. They loved her—that was enough. At least *she* knew that Michael wasn't some mutant leprechaun, that he was flesh and blood. And charm and persuasion . . . with a kiss that made her feel . . .

She didn't need this. With a swipe of fingers through her hair, she tramped into the house, tugging the scarf from around her neck.

Two hours later, the truck's horn called her back outside.

"I tell you, Cathleen, 'twas like a miracle," Uncle Kevin declared, climbing down from the cab. "I thought we'd lose the little fellow, so twisted and backward he was. I couldn't reach to turn him, and the mare she was a frightened lass, kicking and fighting, even though we'd given her something."

Aunt Brigid hissed, "Now, Kevin, don't be filling her head with nonsense again." Curious, Cass followed them in.

"'Tis no nonsense, Brigid. That foal was a goner, I'd wager my betting allowance on it. And then, Cathleen, the mare began to calm like someone was soothing her, like a lover was whispering sweet words into her ear."

"Come along now, Cass. We'll get some food together." Aunt Brigid led her to the kitchen.

Uncle Kevin disappeared into the bedroom. "And *then,* Cathleen," he shouted through the small house, "that foal began to turn. "'Twas as if strong hands were guiding the little fellow right into this world. He slid out neat as could be. A pretty one he is, too."

Her uncle strode into the kitchen pulling a gray flannel shirt over his head, tugging suspenders up to his rounded shoulders. Cass warmed with affection watching the stocky little man. How she loved his full white mustache twitching like a busy caterpiller when he talked.

"Aye, 'tis missing you we're going to be, Cathleen. You mustn't stay away ten years again." He engulfed her in a bear hug, then stood back to look at her.

"That's right, Cass." Her aunt handed her bowls of cold food for the table.

Hiking a chair up, Kevin waited until Brigid and Cass were seated, offered a hurried blessing, then set to scooping large helpings of food onto his plate.

"It's work like that makes a man hungry, I tell you. I hardly feel the food you brought me there, Brigid." He chewed thoughtfully. "I'll bet Mick O'Shea will be eating his fill this evening, too."

Cass's fork clattered to the table.

"Now, Kevin. That's enough," Aunt Brigid scolded. "A shut mouth catches no flies."

"You know Mick O'Shea?" Cass demanded.

"Now, Cass, eat your dinner and don't be listening to that old Irishman." Aunt Brigid spooned more cold potatoes onto Cass's plate.

"No, please, Biddie I'd like to know." To placate her aunt, she retrieved her fork and dug into the mound of food.

"Sure, now, it's what I've been telling you, lass. 'Twas Mick O'Shea delivered that foal, just as he always helps out when there's a problem with the horses. A mighty good hand he is with all the animals, but especially with the horses."

Cass could hardly believe her ears. "He works at the same stud farm *you* do. You've *seen* him work with Hugh Finnegan's horses. You *know* him. That's wonderful."

She smiled, searching for the right words to tell them that this was the person she'd known ten years ago.

"Well, not exactly—"

"Cass," Aunt Brigid interrupted, "he doesn't know Mick O'Shea, and he doesn't work with him. Mick O'Shea is...just another Irish fantasy." Aunt Brigid stood, pushing her chair back with a harsh scrape. "Tell her, Kevin."

He brushed his fingers back and forth across his mustache, glancing out of the top of his eyes at Brigid. Then he shifted toward Cass and began to push food around his plate.

"Sure now, Cathleen, it's like this. Whenever something good happens where it isn't expected, especially with the animals, all over County Kildare, we say it was Mick O'Shea. It's kind of like saying it was a blessing, you understand."

Cass fought to maintain a smile. "So you've never actually seen Micha... Mick O'Shea?"

"No, Cathleen—" he paused, his shoulders raised in an apologetic shrug "—can't truly say that I have. Truth be told, I guess I don't really believe the legend. 'Twas probably the tranquilizer finally helped the mare. But I'd rather say it was a leprechaun any day than a needleful of chemicals in the mare's rump."

Cass stopped herself from saying, "Michael's not a leprechaun." She was obviously losing her mind, but she didn't need to worry her aunt and uncle all over again.

Was it something in the Irish air? Maybe the food? She put her fork down, no longer hungry. Why was it that when she came here she... saw things, she imagined this... person?

She *had* seen him. She'd felt his hands. She'd... tasted his sweet kiss.

Stop. It didn't matter. She was going back to St. Louis tomorrow, back to a reality she was sure of—the security of her job and the possibility of a reasonable relationship with the very *un*-imagined Blake Brockman.

"I...understand, Uncle Kevin." Cass's smile dissolved, and she shifted to telling of her visit to the funeral home, never mentioning Michael.

At last they finished eating, and she helped clear away the dishes. With overwhelming relief, she escaped outside. A walk was what she needed, to clear her head, yet she found herself wandering to the *rath*, thinking of Michael, remembering much too vividly the feel of his mouth on hers.

No, no more adolescent fantasies, she told herself. Michael wasn't real. Uncle Kevin's reluctant admission made that undeniable.

She yanked the red scarf from her pocket and threw it as far as she could. Then she hurried back to the house.

The excitement in the Glinbrendan air seemed almost palpable. Drawers slammed, cupboard doors squeaked, voices full of laughter floated out to Michael through the window. Banned from the house, he wandered back from his stroll, stopping near the door to wait to be called in.

Ah, Glinbrendan, he mused. So well etched in his mind, he could call it up in wonderful detail wherever he was. He was going to miss this place.

Truth was, he couldn't be leaving his work at the stud farm at a better time. The late-season foal had finally struggled into the world, though 'twas a bit of touch and go for a while. Thanks to Aunt Brigid's note, he'd arrived in time to help. The training of the other horses was going well, too, and the two-year-olds were into a regular exercise program.

Only one blemish marred his satisfaction. Saving the foal meant he hadn't been able to keep his promise to Cass. He fingered the red scarf in his pocket, found near the *rath* during his stroll. If it was Cass's, he hoped it didn't mean she'd rejected him. He couldn't lose her faith now, after she'd finally returned.

From the time he'd been old enough to understand, Pegeen had taught him—whatever the risk, he should always follow his heart. She said so still, though it meant sending her firstborn son beyond the shores of Ireland. 'Twas surely the only chance he'd have to win Cass.

"Michael? We're ready," a voice called from inside.

He entered the house and walked to the table. His father sat at the head looking somber, his dark eyebrows drawn together in one furry line. Pegeen stood beside her husband's chair, her small hand resting on his shoulder, her chin held high. The rest of the family sat on either side.

"These are the gifts we give you, Michael, to take into the world." Pegeen pointed to the items of clothing they each held up from stacks in front of them. They'd managed to accumulate quite an assortment. Some even looked new, and more amazing, most appeared as if they would fit.

He scanned round the table with affection. In the faces of his brothers and sisters he saw anticipation and goodwill . . . and only traces of concern.

"And, Michael," his father said, "no O'Shea goes into the world without his own keep."

Each person emptied a pouch onto the table with a clatter. They pushed the money into the center where it made an impressive mound.

"That'll do me just grand," he said, thinking that until now, no O'Shea had gone into the world at all, keep or no.

"This is to carry it in." From his lap, his father produced a wooden box, every inch carved in shamrock designs. Michael had seen him working and smoothing it in the evenings for years. Proudly, his father demonstrated the locking mechanism, which was an intricate puzzle.

"You go with our blessings, Michael." Pegeen's voice wavered. "We hope someday you'll come back to us...with Cathleen." She dabbed at her eyes with the corner of her apron, then dismissed them all with a laugh. "Now, go be getting ready. Sean has a valise for you. And don't be forgetting your cap." Her voice caught and she turned away.

Michael shook his father's hand and kissed Pegeen on both cheeks. The rest of the O'Sheas clamored around to bestow hugs and claps on the back.

In the bedroom, he showed off his new clothes amidst laughter and applause. But his mind kept returning to Cass.

In ten years the lass he'd dreamed of had become a woman, a lovely woman, a woman worth following. And though her spirit seemed all but buried, he still saw traces of what had first captured him, enough to give him hope. Enough to revive a long-banked fire and a dream that only *began* with kisses.

He'd have to treat her very gently out in the world. He didn't want to scare her away. If she stopped believing in him, if she went away from him out there, where would he be? He had no idea, and Pegeen had no answer.

The train's engine roared half an octave higher, rousing people on the platform at Kildare Station to say goodbye.

"Good journey to you, Cathleen, and safe back again to us soon." Uncle Kevin hugged Cass. Aunt Brigid wiped her eyes and handed Cass the package of food she'd prepared.

Reluctantly, Cass boarded. Through the window, she watched them leave while she dabbed her own eyes with the Irish hanky Aunt Brigid had tucked into Cass's navy suit pocket earlier. At last she turned. Juggling her luggage and the package of food, she located her seat and dropped into it.

For a moment she sat, eyes closed, thinking about the importance of the day. She was on her way home, and this time she was taking her father with her. She wanted more than anything to do this, to take her father home. Maybe, by this act of care, she could make up for the unresolved differences between them.

She was bargaining, she knew—part of the process of grieving. She'd come to Ireland too late to heal their rift. Yet maybe, by reuniting her father and mother, by bringing together such opposite influences in her life, she could finally feel at peace with herself.

There was no logic to it. She just knew that this time, even if her father would have chosen a more practical arrangement, she had to follow her feelings.

Opening her eyes, she drew in a deep breath. The sooner they got going, the better, yet people still milled about on the platform outside. Surely the train wouldn't leave late. Please, not this morning. Unable to sit still, she stashed her luggage and strode to exit.

Outside, she shifted from one high heel to the other, watching people say goodbye. No familiar faces here. The only people she knew in Ireland, besides her aunt and uncle, were the O'Sheas, and the O'Sheas didn't exist. The thought hurt, like the unexpected bite of a sliver.

Nonsense. She should be relieved to know with certainty that Michael was *not* among the people at the station.

The assurance did little to quiet her agitation . . . or to ease the sense of something lost.

She walked along the side of the yellow train wondering what was keeping it from leaving, already wishing that she'd worn her running shoes. Nearby, laughter caught her attention, deep-throated and hearty—like Michael's had sounded just yesterday morning at the *rath*.

Stop. It couldn't be Michael. The time had come to put him out of her mind for good.

The train's wheezy horn blasted, and the engine revved higher as if to stir the waiting behemoth into motion.

Finally. Hurrying to the nearest car, she stepped in. A porter pulled the door closed as the train began to move.

At the first empty seat, she stopped. Perching on the armrest, she slipped one shoe off and rubbed her foot, watching a narrow track creep up her leg. Darn. Barely on her way and already she'd run a nylon.

Ahead, a dark curly head leaned out into the aisle. Cass drew in a sharp breath. Dropping her shoe, she straightened. A gap-toothed young man grinned back at her before returning to his newspaper. She let her breath out slowly. Not Michael.

Of course not Michael, and this wasn't the time for an overactive imagination. She needed to deal with reality. Truly annoyed at herself, she shoved a short strand of wayward hair behind an ear and marched down the aisle.

Three cars later, she spotted her luggage. Relieved, she slid through to the window seat, only to stop, hanging in midair like a circus performer poised between trapezes. A faded red bandanna lay in the middle of the seat.

Her scarf! Michael had returned it just yesterday, after he'd . . . kissed her. Heat crept up her neck.

But she'd thrown it away last evening. She was hallucinating again. She was getting hysterical.

She needed to get a grip. Bandannas were all made of the same material. Someone had just left this one behind. Cautiously, she reached to pick it up.

"Sure, you've found your scarf, Cass. I brought it to you this time instead of waiting for you to come after it."

She fell into the seat as if she'd been pushed. "Michael! What are you...? How did you...? How *can* you...?" Then she stopped breathing altogether.

Filling the whole aisle, one hand resting on the seat back, he no longer looked like a stable hand. Country gentleman—that was the first thought that came to her mind. His blue tweed sweater reflected royal blue in his eyes and did little to disguise the breadth of his shoulders. Gray corduroy pants with soft pleats rode his narrow hips, gaving him an air of casual gentility. Every inch of him looked very real, hazardously real.

"Aren't you going to ask me to sit down?"

She stared up at him. "Is this your seat?" She couldn't think of anything else to say. How could he have the seat next to hers? How could he even be here?

"Yes..."

Cass fought to regain her composure. "Let me see your ticket."

"My ticket? Sure, 'twould be in my bag. I'll just dig it out, since you're not wanting to believe." He pointed to a tapestry-covered bag under the window seat.

"Never mind, Michael. Just sit down." She didn't want to get into an argument about believing. She stood to let him through, holding the back of the seat to steady herself against the train's rocking.

The train swayed, and Michael reached for her. She lunged into the compact wall of his chest and felt the steadying warmth of his arm as it circled her. Her heart collided with her ribs.

"Wait...Michael." Breathless, she tried to push away. "Why—why are you here?" she stammered, trying to ignore the feel of his solid body inch for inch against hers. "I told you...I don't need your help," she insisted, trying to deny the woodsy scent of his wool sweater mingled with his own masculinity. "I don't want you to go with me."

The ride smoothed out, and she shoved back, dropping into the seat. Her hands shook.

"Now, Cass, there's no law that says we can't ride on the same train together. Would you choose to sit by yourself when there's a friend riding in the same car? That doesn't seem very neighborly." His smile deepened.

Neighborly? She didn't know what she was feeling, but she was pretty sure it wasn't neighborly. Her heart seemed on the verge of cardiac arrest. She waved him into his seat by the window, afraid to look at him again. "Wait. You'd better find that ticket, because the porter's coming."

"The porter? Yes. Hmm...I didn't seem to be finding the ticket now, did I?" He patted his trouser pockets.

"Michael, I don't believe you have a ticket. What are you up to? Where do you think you're going?"

"I'm going to America. I'm going to work in America."

"You're...?" No. Not with her. She wouldn't spend more time with him. Being with Michael would only lead to...something unpredictable. Something terribly threatening to her hard-won rational life.

She was overreacting. Too many things were coming at her too fast. Her responses to Michael were out of proportion, all of them, and her feelings were out of control. If she didn't calm down, she'd make a fool of herself. She better move. To another seat. In another car. She shifted to stand up.

"Excuse me, miss." The porter blocked her escape. "I need to check your ticket."

Shakily, Cass dug hers out and handed it to him.

"Sir, I seem to have lost my ticket," Michael said, "but I'll be happy to purchase another. To Dublin, if you don't mind." He tugged the tapestry-covered bag from under his seat, unsnapped the catch and pulled the sides open.

Cass saw a stack of neatly folded clothes inside, on top of which laid a wonderfully carved wooden box.

"'Tis beautiful, isn't it?" Michael said, lifting the box out. He manipulated several side panels and slid the lid open. Inside lay a mound of money.

Cass blinked to keep from staring. The box was almost full. Faded bills lay jumbled with a crazy assortment of coins, many of which gleamed a dull bronze. Surely they weren't gold. She looked away, embarrassed at her nosiness.

A reaction quickly forgotten when she glanced out the window. The train had slowed almost to a crawl. Something was wrong.

Unperturbed, Michael and the porter seemed totally engrossed in counting money, the porter selecting from among the variety of coins until he was satisfied.

"Have a pleasant trip, sir."

Cass caught the porter's arm. "Please, do you happen to know why we're stopping?"

"Lass, all I do is make sure folks are on the train—" his grin broadened to include Michael "—and that they have a ticket. Nevertheless, I do believe they were doing some work on the tracks earlier." He touched his cap and proceeded down the aisle.

"Oh, dear."

"Cass, is there a problem?"

She looked up at the concern in Michael's voice. "I hope not. It's just that Mr. Donovan's hand-wringing didn't exactly fill me with confidence. According to him, anything could go wrong."

"Don't worry, Cass. I'll help you. When we get to Dublin, I'll help you with whatever problem there is."

If we ever get to Dublin, she thought, but the melody of Michael's brogue and the empathy she found in his face calmed her.

Perhaps she could share the trip into Dublin with him after all. And if they arrived late, maybe she should take him up on his offer of help. He owed her that much since he hadn't cleared her reputation with her aunt and uncle. She could consider his help repayment of an obligation. When she was sure that she and her father's casket were leaving Dublin together, she would part ways with Michael.

In the meantime, she'd have to find neutral ground. "How is your family, Michael? Your sister Fiona?" She sat back and tried to relax as the train slowly picked up speed.

"Ah, lovely Fiona. She liked you very much, Cass. She's married now, with twins of her own. Brieda and Brendan, and grand ones they are, too."

Married...with children. Of course. Fiona was her age. A lot of women were married and raising a family by the time they were twenty-seven. They weren't career women like herself, or career women with families like her best friend, Jenn.

"What about you, Michael?"

"No, I've not married, Cass," he answered quietly.

"I didn't mean . . ." She had no reason to feel pleased. "I mean, tell me about your job offer in America." She hadn't meant to ask that, either, but she couldn't call the words back.

He seemed to weigh his answer. "There's a brewery by the name of Anheuser-Busch. They've sponsored our big annual horse race the last few years. The Derby."

"Michael, that brewery's in St. Louis."

"Sure, Cass, and they have these magnificent animals called Clydesdales. They were Scottish horses originally but we . . . Irish have the touch for working with them."

"No."

"Cass, the Irish are known the world over for their fine horses. You cannot deny—"

"I mean . . . surely you're not going to St. Louis to work."

He considered her a moment before answering. "I understand St. Louis is a big city, Cass. If it's me you're worrying about seeing, you needn't fret. When we part ways, you'll never know I'm around."

"Good." She pushed back in her seat and clapped her arms across her chest. Darn him. The last thing she needed at home was a man who left her seriously in question of her reason, who stirred unrealistic feelings.

Blake Brockman was the only man she intended to involve in her life. Blake was like her father—all reality and common sense and right answers.

But . . . She drew in a deep breath and let it out slowly. She had to admit Michael was right. St. Louis was a big city. Lots of people could live there and never cross paths. And working with the beautiful Clydesdales was an opportunity few horse lovers could turn down. She was just acting petty. Her emotions were out of kilter.

She would stop acting like a spoiled brat. She was a grown woman now, not a smitten teenager. She'd pull herself together so, when the time came, they could at least part on congenial terms.

Unfolding her arms, she leaned toward him. "When do you leave for the States, Michael?" His face showed no signs of the coolness she'd imagined.

"Sure now, I do not know yet."

"You don't know?" A suspicion nudged her. "Michael, you haven't bought a plane ticket yet?"

"A plane ticket? No, not yet."

"Do you have a passport?"

"A passport?"

"Do you have any money besides what's in that box?"

"No, Cass, that's my whole fortune."

She muttered something under her breath. Once they arrived at Dublin airport, she could lose Michael in the crowd. He'd never get his arrangements made in time to leave Ireland on the same flight she did. Especially if he had no passport.

Then she would never see him again.

Or, as he had done with her, she could offer to help.

Chapter Four

Heuston Station in Dublin bustled with travelers. Michael followed Cass, stopping to stare at the high ceiling, to watch so many people rushing across the broad floor. He'd never seen such a grand sight.

"Are you coming, Michael?"

"Aye, Cass." And he'd have to hurry if he wanted to catch up to her before she raced outside. He'd seen that expression before—a woman with her mind made up. She was set on looking after her father by herself. Sure, she must have loved him as much as Wil loved her, even though they hadn't always seen eye to eye.

'Twas a shame Wil died before she knew how he'd changed. Someday Michael would tell her—when she learned to trust him again. Right now, though, her belief in him was too shaky. He'd best let her have her head.

Just as he followed her out the door, he heard, "Miss Cathleen Kohlmann. Report to ticket window three." The words echoed behind him through the station.

"They're paging me?"

She looked to him for confirmation, and he saw the concern in her eyes. Hefting their luggage a little higher, he followed her back inside, letting his gaze linger on her small figure. Such a determined wee thing. If only she'd let him help.

Cass stopped in front of a counter and spoke to the bald man standing behind it. "I'm Cathleen Kohlmann. You paged me?"

"Aye, Miss Kohlmann, there's a phone call for you."

What manner of summons was this? Michael wondered. He kept pace with Cass as they followed the man into a room shut off from the bustle and echo of the station. A large woman beckoned to them while she spoke into a black instrument.

"Miss Kohlmann? You have a call. A Mr. Donovan."

Michael saw Cass's fair skin grow pale and her hand tremble when she reached for the phone.

"Mr. Donovan? This is Cathleen Kohlmann." She listened, then flinched and held the phone away from her ear.

"Can you hear me, Miss Kohlmann?"

Not only Cass, but everyone in the room could hear Mr. Donovan. Michael pictured the wizened old man shouting at a similar instrument held away from his mouth.

"I can hear you, Mr. Donovan. What's the matter? Has something happened to the casket?"

Even a few feet away, Michael heard Mr. Donovan's heartfelt sigh, saw the fear it fanned in Cass's eyes.

"Ah, Miss Kohlmann. We had a bit of a problem with the hearse. The trials and tribulations I've been through, I've hardly the energy to tell you. First, we ran a bit short of the petrol. Then the driver got tied up at the road works, you know, and slid into a rut. The axle broke, and what with the fog and all, well, we had to transfer your father, may he rest in peace, to a lorry, which was no small task since the casket weighs more than a few men can carry. Especially in a box with no handles. I'm telling you—"

"Mr. Donovan," she interrupted. "Where's my father now?"

"I was about to tell you, Miss Kohlmann. The truck got away but a short while ago, and I sent it straight to the airport. Sure to God, Miss Kohlmann, it will be nothing but His Divine Intervention that will get your father to America. He should have stayed here to rest in peace, as I've said many a time."

Michael saw his own concern mirrored in Cass's eyes.

"Does the driver know the departure time?" Cass asked.

"Aye, Miss Kohlmann, I gave him the information, and he'll be there. He's my nephew, the driver is, Brian Donovan by name. Named after me by my brother, God bless him. So I give you my word on it. I do not like handling your father this way, Miss Kohlmann, but I'll make good our agreement. God bless, Miss Kohlmann."

"Mr. Donovan?" She shook the receiver. "He hung up!"

Michael took the instrument from her. Her hand felt cold to his touch. "It's relieved you must be feeling, Cass," he said, though she didn't look relieved. She looked worried but determined, and he was glad to see a spark in her eyes as she hurried through the door.

He caught up with her halfway through the station. "Whoa, Cass. Hold up. You're outrunning me, and you're not even properly shod. Where might you be going?"

"I told you before, I don't need your help."

"You're more stubborn than Pegeen," he said, hiking a piece of luggage under his arm and lengthening his stride to keep up with her. "Sure, the man who made time made plenty of it. I do not understand the rush, Cass."

"Let me spell it out. My father's body isn't embalmed. That means—" her voice caught, but she continued "—his casket has to be on the flight today. I'll feel a lot better when I know he's at the airport. He could still be in Kildare, or on the road to Cork or Limerick or—"

"Easy, Cass. Slow down, now. Don't be getting yourself all upset."

"I'm not upset, I'm . . . I'm going to the airport."

"Then I'll be going with you," he said quietly.

His words seemed to slow her if only for an instant, and he thought he saw a bit of gratitude . . . of something more than gratitude before her eyes ebbed to the muted gray of pewter. Not much to build his hope, but 'twould have to do for now.

"Come on, Michael. The cabs are over there." Cass pointed to the three vehicles parked along the curb.

"Tax-i?" he seemed to test the word written on the car. "So they are. I'll see if one of them is for hire."

"They're all for hire. Let's get the first one."

Cass slid inside the vehicle, and Michael climbed in beside her. Closing her eyes, she tried to quiet the feelings that tumbled along with her heartbeat. She mustn't worry about her father. Mr. Donovan had assured her that his casket was on its way to the airport. And she mustn't let Michael affect her this way.

She looked at him through half-closed eyes and then couldn't stop looking. He viewed the streets of Dublin with the pure wonder of a child, his face filled with awe and pleasure. She felt again a jolt, a response to him that came unexpected and almost stopped her heart, just as she felt an uninvited attraction every time he offered help in his soft persuasive brogue. Darn, she didn't need this man in her life. Why hadn't he just stayed disappeared?

She had to stop this. She needed to locate her father at the airport, show Michael where to buy his ticket and then be on her way. She needed to get Michael out of her life so she could focus on her father.

She sat up straighter. "All right, Michael. What about your passport?" She dug out her own and handed it to him. "Do you have one of these? Because if you don't, you might as well go right back to Glinbrendan, or wherever it is you live. You can't travel internationally without one."

Michael took the document and flipped through the pages. On the inside of the blue cover, he discovered Cass's photograph. The corner of his mouth tugged into a half grin. "Ah yes, documents."

"Then you do have a passport." She looked at him more closely. She didn't think an imaginary creature could obtain a passport. A passport would prove he was real.

"Is it valid? Let me see."

His smile deepened. "I cannot, Cass."

"Why not, for heaven's sake?"

"It's under my clothing, and I don't think you would want me to fetch it right now." His eyes teased. "Unless, of course, you insist." He reached for his belt.

"No. I'll take your word for it." She busied herself by putting her passport away to hide the heat in her cheeks. "First thing when we get to the airport, I'll confirm my arrangements, and then we'll— Oh, your money. Where did you get that money? Why didn't you buy traveler's checks?''

She didn't wait for an answer. "Are you sure you have enough? You'll have to change to American money, you know. Let's see what you have."

He pulled the box from his suitcase and opened it. Without warning, he tipped the contents into the lap of her navy blue skirt. "This is all that I have, Cass."

At the sound of the cascading coins, the driver's head swiveled, the taxi swerved and Cass jostled across the seat. Coins and bills flew around them, but all she could see was Michael's periwinkle blue sweater, all she could feel was his solid chest.

She looked up to the deeper blue of his eyes and saw both surprise and pleasure there. Breathless, she watched him scan her face, his eyes filled with questions as they drifted to her lips. She waited, trembling, wanting his kiss even as her mind shouted a warning.

His lips brushed hers, asking, inviting, and when she didn't pull away, he bent to close the breathless space between them, requesting more, seeking her taste, igniting heat that glowed brighter as his kiss fanned to flame. She didn't want to stop him, didn't want to stop herself . . .

But she must.

She pushed away and saw disappointment flicker across his face, and something else . . . was it concern? Before she could even think, he leaned to collect money from the floor.

Suddenly she felt very alone, and somehow . . . abandoned. She struggled to right herself, torn between shock and regret. Michael's kiss had stirred her, had ignited her. She wanted to kiss him back.

No. She didn't want this. These kinds of unwieldy emotions had no place in her life. They only ended in pain.

"Now look what you've done, Michael," she said, hunting for scattered coins to mask her shattered feelings.

The taxi driver cleared his throat noisily. "Dublin Airport ahead."

She helped Michael gather the last of the coins, rubbing the heavier pieces between her fingers, wondering at their golden glow. Had she just yielded to a leprechaun?

The driver pulled to a stop in front of the terminal and helped unload their bags. Cass snatched hers up and walked to the doors without a word. Michael followed her to the Aer Lingus counter where she dumped her bags onto the slide-through scales. He did the same with his.

"You'll have to get your ticket before you check your bag, Michael," Cass said.

He smiled at the blond woman behind the counter and made no move to retrieve the suitcase.

All right then, just let his bag get lost. Cass handed her ticket and papers to the uniformed woman.

After checking them carefully, the agent handed the documents back. "Everything is fine, Miss Kohlmann. The casket hasn't arrived yet, but there's space for it. It'll be loaded as soon as it comes. Here's your boarding pass. Have a comfortable flight."

The clock on the wall showed just past ten-thirty. Surely the truck should be here by now. Cass tried to ignore a stab of concern. After all, the plane didn't leave until noon. She shouldn't worry—yet.

"I would like a ticket, too." Michael interrupted her thoughts. "Just like Miss Kohlmann's. All the way to St. Louis in America, with a seat next to hers."

About as likely as winning the lottery, Cass thought. Michael's artlessness amazed her. His smile, though, was enough to melt ice, although the ticket agent was hardly acting icy. Cass experienced a twinge in her midsection. Probably hunger from not eating breakfast. Her feet hurt, too.

"Michael, I'm going to sit down," she told him. He obviously didn't need her help, and she didn't want to see his disappointment when the woman denied his request. Nor did she want to know his alternative arrangements.

He caught her arm. "Where are you going, Cass?"

"Just over there to that bench."

He looked to where she pointed, and his hand loosened, his anxious expression relaxed.

When she reached the bench, she turned to find him watching her, as she'd expected, his look setting something inside of her fluttering. But as soon as he made eye contact, he turned back to the ticket agent who smiled up at him warmly.

Cass should have known. An attractive man like Michael no doubt expected the attentions of women. Just look at the way he flirted. He probably acted that way with every woman. All the more reason for her to part ways with him.

Irritated, she sat and opened the package her aunt had prepared. The bundle contained exactly what she needed, cheese and homemade bread—a little protein, a few carbohydrates—to get things back into perspective. She was suffering from low blood sugar and jet lag, that was all. And grief.

Now for her shoes. From the bottom of her tote, she pulled pink-and-white running shoes and slipped them on. A touch of lip gloss, and she'd be ready to handle anything.

"Cass?" Michael beckoned her to the counter.

"We'll need your signature, Miss Kohlmann." The ticket agent was all efficiency. "We can't accept Mr. O'Shea's currency, so he suggested the ticket be paid for in the same manner as yours, which is, of course, on your charge."

"What?"

"We had to do some juggling, but we managed to put Mr. O'Shea next to you all the way to St. Louis."

Cass couldn't believe her ears. "*We* managed," the woman had said, as if she and Michael were some kind of reservations team. And what they'd accomplished was impossible. Surely Michael had worked some kind of spell.

The woman's scrutiny bordered on downright nosiness. But Michael's grin warmed like a ray of Irish sun. Cass took the woman's pen reluctantly... and signed.

"Thank you, Miss Kohlmann. Your bags are all checked." The agent returned her attention to Michael. "Come back to Ireland soon, Mr. O'Shea. And you, too, Miss Kohlmann."

Cass strode toward the gate without a backward glance. Michael's ticket must have cost a fortune. *Her* fortune. She hardly knew Michael O'Shea, yet she'd just committed a lot of hard-earned money so he could travel to America. She'd been too stunned to check how much. He was handsome and charming, and she was grieving and out of control.

Michael fell into step with her. "The lass said I could sell my coins for American dollars when we get there, Cass, so I can repay you. She reminded me of my sister Penelope, the woman did. Fixed things with hardly a bother. Now I can be sure that you and Wil are safe all the way to St. Louis."

"Wil?" She slowed at his use of her father's name, then stopped abruptly. "My father!" She checked her watch. "He should be here by now." She glared up at Michael, torn between fear and anger. She'd let him tie himself to her with the promise of help and a debt of gold coins. She'd let him stir her feelings. "Okay, Michael, you just sold yourself into servitude. Come with me."

She turned back toward the ticket counter only to be stopped by another blaring request. "Cathleen Kohlmann, report to the Aer Lingus ticket counter."

"You paged me?" Cass asked when she reached the ticket agent. She was out of breath from the sprint. "What is it? What's the matter?"

"There's a call from a Mr. Brian Donovan. He says he's had an accident with his truck."

Cass reached for the phone. "Brian Donovan? This is Cass Kohlmann. Where are you?"

She reeled at the words of the young man on the end of the line. "There's no way you can get your truck going? Isn't there another vehicle you could hire?" Her heart sank at his answer. "How far from the airport are you? A couple of kilometers?" Less than two miles.

"Let me talk to him." Michael sounded more serious than Cass had ever heard him. "Tell Brian Donovan it's me."

"Brian, I'm going to let you talk to Michael O'Shea."

Michael placed the receiver carefully to his ear. "This is Michael O'Shea, can you hear me?"

The tension around his eyes relaxed as he launched a stream of rapid-fire questions. "We'll be there soon, Brian. Come, Cass. We're going to get your father."

Outside the terminal, he paused and looked around.

"Michael, what are you doing?" Cass pleaded.

"Looking for the road to your father."

"The taxi driver will know." Please know, she prayed.

"Ah, yes. Tax-i." He followed her into the back of the nearest cab. "We'd be needing your fastest trip to the Boot Inn," he told the driver.

The Boot Inn? She hoped Michael had it right. She hoped she hadn't given leave of her senses again—taking a taxi into the countryside of Ireland in search of a lost casket—with a person she wasn't at all sure was real.

The road doglegged, then diminished to a narrower route that led to a cluster of buildings. As the taxi drew nearer, a crowd of people spread out to reveal a big American car, one fender crumpled like used aluminum foil. A dilapidated truck slumped into the damage, its bent hood open like a hungry bird, its tire tilted at a painful angle.

Cass's hopes plunged. Brian Donovan was right. The truck was beyond salvaging in time to make the trip to the airport. Michael would need a miracle to help.

The cab stopped, and Michael pulled Cass out after him. Beckoning to the lanky, orange-haired boy slouched against the truck, Michael led Cass across the road to a throng of men heatedly debating who was to blame for the accident.

"Gentlemen," he interrupted. "The lovely lady is Cathleen O'Neil Kohlmann, and her father, may he rest in peace, is in the back of that truck." The man quieted to stare at them. Several removed their caps.

"Wil Kohlmann must be at the airport by noon," Michael continued. "Two pints of stout for those who'll bear the pall to the airport." He pulled money from his pockets. "And an extra pint if we make it in time." He handed the money to a man in a bib apron, then strode to the truck.

Cass watched in amazement as Michael jumped into the back with several men behind. Their voices emerged in unison, "One, two, heave," and from the end of the truck, a box stenciled with the name KOHLMANN slid into the sunlight.

Quickly, five men lined up on either side, and when the count sounded again, they hoisted the box onto their shoulders. With stifled grunts, they moved forward.

Unbelievable, Cass thought. Michael was working a miracle after all.

The taxi drove slowly down the middle of the road. It was followed by ten men carrying the casket, Michael and the orange-haired boy in front. A second crew of men and a mixture of women and children brought up the rear. Brushing away tears, Cass ran to catch up.

Michael began to sing, and soon everyone joined in, their voices enthusiastic if not all on key, their feet falling into a rhythm that set them marching at a good pace. By the time they reached the airline terminal, they'd drawn a crowd.

Cass ran ahead to activate the doors. The clock inside read quarter to twelve. They were going to make it!

People in airline uniforms directed the parade through the terminal. Cass hurried to rejoin Michael. At the cargo dock, she waited while he helped the men lift the casket onto a freight vehicle. When it was secured, he returned.

"You go find our seats on the airplane, Cass. I'll stay here until I see your father on board."

She hesitated. She had no reason to doubt Michael now. She knew he would take care of her father. Her reluctance sprang from something else. She didn't want to go without him.

"Do you have your boarding pass?"

He nodded, his smile gentle.

"Don't forget to...retrieve your passport." She turned away, then paused. "And hurry, Michael."

"Aye, Cass."

His lopsided grin lingered in her mind all the way back to the terminal. It disturbed her that Michael hadn't come with her. It surprised her even more that she cared.

She'd misjudged him. No magic and miracles. Just cleverness and generosity had helped him rescue her father. In spite of her protests, he'd stayed with her to help.

But—a firm voice prodded her—she mustn't let gratitude distort her feelings. Gratitude was appropriate. Caution continued to be a very good idea. But any other feelings for Michael were simply not part of her game plan.

She boarded the plane, taking note of all the empty spaces. Michael hadn't used magic to get on this flight, either. Finding their seats, she slid across to the window and looked out. Below, workmen emptied baggage carts.

She checked her watch. Exactly twelve noon. Where was Michael? She saw a woman up front shove down the aisle with her luggage. Outside, the jetbridge drew back slowly from the side of the plane. They'd closed the plane door.

They were leaving. She was leaving...without Michael. Without saying goodbye. Again. She hadn't even thanked him for his help. In spite of the feelings he stirred in her, in spite of the fact that she didn't want him interfering in her life, she hadn't intended to just walk away without expressing her...appreciation.

She couldn't even write to him. How could she send a letter to a man who lived in a town no one had heard of? The thought touched an old wound deep inside.

Maybe the whole escapade with the broken-down truck and the casket parade was just another of her fantasies.

Maybe she'd been on the plane the whole time, waiting for it to leave, and had fallen asleep. Maybe she'd dreamed it all.

Reaching down, she pushed off her running shoes and rubbed her burning feet. Darn, her last pair of nylons was completely shot. Only one explanation accounted for her ruined nylons and her aching feet, and it had nothing to do with dreams and fantasies—and a whole lot to do with jogging across Ireland rescuing her father with an unpredictable Irishman who had a propensity to disappear.

The plane moved backward. Quickly she searched the tarmac outside for his familiar figure. No one was there. She stretched to view the inside aisle. Empty.

Well. She shoved back into the seat, denying the emptiness where her heart was supposed to be. She'd wanted Michael O'Shea out of her life, and apparently she'd gotten her wish. She should be glad for one less worry. Now she could relax and get some sleep.

She snatched the pillow from the vacant seat and shoved it into the niche by the window. Curling up, she pressed her eyes shut and waited for the plane to leave the ground.

"Cass, are you asleep?" Michael whispered, sitting down beside her. Much to his relief, her eyes flew open.

"Michael! Where have you been?"

"Putting my passport away."

He hadn't wanted to wake her. Sure, she looked so unhappy, her fair face frowning so, even a tear at the corner of her eye. The task of taking her father home was bearing heavy upon her. 'Twas good he was with her. And there for a moment, before she'd had time to think, she'd looked truly glad to see him. More than anything, he wanted her to be glad to see him.

Outside the window the ground flew by, stealing his attention. His pulse leaped. He leaned closer to see out, but an invisible force pressed against his body.

"Michael, what are you doing? Fasten your seat belt."

The roar in his ears increased, the pressure against his body grew. He saw the ground fall away beneath them. St. Paddy in heaven, he was flying! A rush of exhilaration hit. 'Twas sheer power he was feeling. No horse had ever raced so forcefully.

A soft touch grazed his leg, drawing him back to where Cass fumbled in the space between them. He reached to help her, their fingers tangling, hers cool and damp in his grasp. She tugged to free herself, but he held her, the rush inside him more exciting still, making him forget caution. He waited to see what she would do.

"Your seat belt, Michael. See that sign?" She pointed to the lighted picture above their heads. He held her hand, watching with pleasure the pink that colored her cheeks, remembering her yielding response to his earlier kiss.

"Look, Michael." She tugged her hand away and pointed to her lap. "Like in the car. You have to wear it to fly."

Her imploring voice jarred his conscience. He was pushing her again. Quickly he searched for the straps and brought the metal parts together with a click. When he looked up for approval, she'd turned away to the window.

So much for thinking Cass was glad to see him. Sure, he had to admit, most of her reactions to him weren't very encouraging. The thought stirred a fleeting sadness. Ten years with no stories and no make-believe had cost her dearly. Her gray eyes hardly ever shone. She'd learned far too many things to worry about, knew far too many rules.

Although right now, he wouldn't mind a few rules himself. In Ireland, at least, he had a good idea of what to expect. What happened when they left remained to be seen. He hoped being seen was exactly what would continue to happen.

No one had ever tested that question before. If one's life were a legend, what happened to that life outside the land of the story? Would he become just another mortal? Would he cease to exist altogether? Or might he be tied to this woman who believed the legend without realizing she did?

The legend offered love as the tie to be sought, but there were many other kinds of tethers, he reminded himself. Sure, he felt something between him and Cass. When he'd kissed her in the taxi, for a moment she'd kissed him back with all the heat of a woman. But she'd not call that any such fancy name as love. An ongoing spell of unpredictable weather, she might admit to, but certainly not love. It wasn't in her rules to love a fantasy. He doubted if the rules she'd learned even allowed desire. And what he felt for her had a great deal to do with desire.

All the same, rules or no, he was here. He'd left Glinbrendan by choice, to seek his dream as Pegeen had taught him. To seek the love of Cass.

Whatever the outcome, he'd ride this race to the end. But he'd have to be careful. He'd have to keep her believing, because without her belief, he'd disappear, and an invisible rider might never cross the finish line.

He turned to look out the window and stared at what he saw. "A down coverlet. Whipped cream on an Irish whiskey. No, the head on a pint of Guinness stout."

"What are you talking about, Michael?"

"I cannot believe what I'm seeing. What am I seeing, Cass?" He leaned for a better view, his shoulder resting comfortably against hers.

Shadowing his movements, Cass leaned away from his touch. His sudden contact only magnified her confusion at the happiness she'd felt when she'd opened her eyes and found him in the seat next to her.

Looking out, she saw what he questioned, a sea of clouds stretching to the horizon. "Be careful, Michael, because what you see is just like heaven. St. Paddy might not like you calling it foam on beer." She tried to sound at ease, to find her way back to neutral ground.

"I should have known. 'Tis beautiful." He settled back into his seat, a smile lingering around his mouth.

Out of the corner of her eye, Cass studied him, realizing that to do so was folly, but unable to stop herself. In profile, his eyelashes were sinfully thick. The slight irregularity in the bridge of his nose made her wonder if it might once have been broken and left to mend without setting. She'd never really studied the straight line of his jaw, or the squareness of his chin—a chin that could well invite a blow from a defensive Irish fist. He did have a few scars, scars that begged to be touched, just like the mole at the corner of his mouth. His full straight mouth that had kissed her so...

She felt suddenly warm. She sat very still, forcing her gaze back to the window, to the cool isolation of the clouds, while she waited for the heat to subside.

This had to stop. She and Michael had a business arrangement, nothing more. He'd helped her with her father, and she'd helped him with his ticket. As soon as he paid her back, it would be bye-bye Irishman.

She sat up straight and addressed him formally, reluctant to look into those twilight blue eyes. "Michael, I didn't thank you properly for all your help with my father."

Michael turned to her, the planes of his face eased into understanding, something akin to amusement in the cant of his eyebrow. Something that flustered her, that sent a wave of warmth spiraling through her veins, that played the memory of his kiss along her lips. She didn't understand what was happening to her.

"Uh, the way you handled all those people at the pub was ... very decisive, Michael. You showed real management—"

"Decisive? Management?" There was laughter in his voice, now. "You sound a bit like your fath—"

Cass looked up at his sudden silence.

"I mean, Cass, that you must have learned such language from your father who was a businessman, wasn't he?"

His face hadn't changed except for the surprise in his eyes. Suddenly, she remembered words he'd spoken earlier.

"You called my father Wil. Michael, did you know him?"

"He came to visit your aunt and uncle often, especially the last year or so." He held her gaze, but she could sense his disquiet. "Your uncle talked about him often at the stud farm. I guess I felt comfortable with his name."

"And also with how he spoke? I find that hard to believe. You sounded as if you were friends, which is highly unlikely since my aunt and uncle deny that you even exist. My uncle told me so again just *yesterday*."

The old anguish welled up. Who was this man sitting beside her? And what was he doing to her? Her father was the last person on earth who would have befriended Michael. He never would have believed. Not realistic, logical Willem Kohlmann.

But if *she* didn't believe the legends, either, that meant Michael was just another man. In which case her uncle could have known Michael after all. But he hadn't. How could she explain that contradiction?

She was too tired and too confused to try to understand. More importantly, the answer simply didn't matter anymore. No matter what kind of spell Michael was working on her, he would soon be out of her life. She rubbed her temples, stroked strands of hair behind her ear. She was getting a headache. She needed to eat. She needed to go home.

Chapter Five

Pressure built in Michael's ears. He felt more than heard a heavy thump beneath him. Glancing at Cass, he expected alarm, but she didn't seem a bit concerned. She was smothering a yawn.

"Shannon," she said. "We stop here for an hour. You can get off if you want. There's a big duty-free shop."

She no longer sounded upset at him, either, although he'd prefer any show of feeling to this painful coolness.

He searched for a way to break through her shuttered expression. If only he could risk telling her more about her father, about the change in him, about the friendship he and Wil had shared. But she wasn't ready to believe that yet, and he couldn't risk losing all credibility with her.

Taking care not to touch her, he looked out at the rolling green landscape, the slate-colored clouds. The earth rose beneath them until they jounced against it.

When the plane stopped, Cass jumped to her feet. "I'm going in. If you get off, be sure to take your boarding pass."

"Wait, Cass. I'll come, too." He'd have a serious problem if he lost sight of her here, but once inside, he might chance it on his own. It would be good for him to find out what happened when he was away from her, although 'twould not be a true test while they were still on Irish soil.

At the shop entrance, Cass looked at her watch. "If you're not here in half an hour, I'll see you on the plane."

He touched the brim of an imaginary cap and held the door, not daring to smile at her efficiency. She looked so cursedly queenly, just like his sister Fiona. Always haughty when things hurt most inside. Ah, Cass, he thought, feeling her grief much more than his own.

Inside the huge market space he kept close tabs on her while he ambled from one merchant to the next. She made a purchase, then hurried through a door marked with a stick figure in a skirt.

Now was his chance. Sparkling light in a glass case had caught his attention. Stepping closer, he discovered shimmering hearts dangling from golden chains and tiny animals shining with the colors of the rainbow. Behind the case, a motherly sort of woman polished long-stemmed goblets.

He cleared his throat, but the woman remained intent on polishing the delicate vessels. Across the room, he saw Cass come back into the market.

"Oh, excuse me, sir. I didn't see you. May I help you?" the merchant woman asked.

Interesting! He watched Cass blend into the crowd. Now what would happen?

"I was looking for a star," he answered.

"We have some." The woman placed a box on the counter. "Is it for someone special?"

"Yes." The truth of his answer warmed him. A lass whose heart believed was very special. "I'll take this one," he said, pointing to a particularly lovely necklace. A cluster of light to sparkle at her throat, as he hoped she would sparkle again, too, before long.

To his dismay he found only a few coins in his pockets. "I've left my money on the airplane. I'll be right back."

If Cass would just stay in the shop long enough. He hurried out and down the corridor. No one looked up when he moved through the line queued at the checkpoint. No one saw him run onto the plane.

None of the seats near his were occupied. Gratified, he retrieved his box and slid the panels. A handful of coins should be enough, he judged, stuffing them into his pockets.

Thankful that Cass wasn't in the corridor, he pushed through the market doors and searched for her inside. No sign of her short red hair. She had to be here somewhere. He wanted to buy the tiny star, but without her...

He *could* just take it. In County Kildare things were often taken, though only as wages for work done. Here 'twould be petty thievery, and Michael O'Shea didn't steal.

He touched the dainty star on the counter and watched tiny flecks of light dance on its five points. The merchant woman continued to polish goblets.

Where the devil was Cass? He turned just in time to see her about to leave.

"Cass!" She would notice his waving arms, wouldn't she?

She hesitated, then stopped. Her rain-gray eyes met his.

"Wait for me, will you?" he called.

He hurried to the counter. "How much do you need?" He held out both hands, full of coins. The woman studied him with suspicion.

"I caught me a leprechaun," he said with a wink. "Are you that amazed that you cannot help me count it out?"

Hesitantly, the woman counted out the money, occasionally rapping a coin on the counter.

"They're real, sure, and if you don't hurry I'll be missing my airplane."

At last he stuffed the tissue-wrapped treasure into his pocket and strode over to Cass.

"An Irishman buying Irish souvenirs? You could probably get these things for a lot less at home, you know." There she went, meddling in his personal affairs when she should be keeping things impersonal.

"Cost is no object when it's for someone special."

Cass shivered inside at the softness of his voice. So Michael did have someone special. Did legendary folks have lovers? she wondered. The word darkened her already lowered spirits. If they were Irish, they probably did, especially a man like Michael. County Kildare was probably full of women who chased him.

She walked beside him to the plane, listening to his airy whistle. The tune wandered sweet and melodic, sliding in and out of a minor key that touched a hidden sadness in her.

At their seats, she stepped back allowing him to enter first. "You sit by the window, Michael. I've flown lots of times."

Obviously pleased, he moved across. Cass dropped into the aisle seat, her foot bumping something underneath. "Michael, your box—"

"Aye, Cass. I came back to get some money."

"You came all the way back while I was in the airport? I didn't see you leave. How'd you do that so fast?" She knew the minute she asked that she wouldn't get a straight answer. "Never mind. It doesn't matter."

She leaned back and closed her eyes. The time had come to make some serious resolutions. She would pretend she was sitting next to a stranger. She would talk only if he spoke, and then she would reply with very short answers. She wouldn't look at him. She wouldn't even think about him. Starting now.

From her tote she removed the book of Irish legends she'd promised Jenny's kids, Annie and Todd. She opened it and began to read—with her eyes. Her mind refused to follow. She was too much aware of Michael.

"Look, Cass, I can see the ocean. I can see waves. And boats. Look how small." He grasped her arm and pulled her toward the window. His hand felt warm. His nearness triggered the same tumbling inside she'd fought before.

"Yes..." She cleared her throat. "I've seen it." She leaned away from him a bit.

"Ah, but it's so beautiful. How can you not look every chance you get?"

The view was beautiful. And Michael's pleasure was irresistible.

"Look, Cass. We're leaving Ireland. There's nothing but ocean out there. I cannot believe there is so much water in this world." He paused. "We're no longer in Ireland," he said quietly. "Can you see how excited I am?"

His hand closed around hers, warm and enfolding with a gentleness that made time stop, that sent heat coursing through her. She forced herself to look at his azure eyes, so filled with anticipation and—could it possibly be—uncertainty?

He seemed to search for words. "It's you that's made this possible for me, you know." For a moment, something different lit his face, something new darkened his eyes, threatening to weaken her resolve.

She sat motionless, her hand still enfolded in his. Whatever Michael was doing to her, she wouldn't, she couldn't think about it.

"Cass? Are you all right?" Alarm flashed across his face. He squeezed her hand, and she felt her pulse quicken.

Carefully, she smiled. She wouldn't let him see the desire he'd stirred. "I'm glad you're excited, Michael. I hope it turns out to be all you expect."

With a deep intake of air, he pressed her hand again. "It will, Cass. I'm sure of that now."

Thank goodness for all the activity on overseas flights, Cass thought. It helped make the hours pass. Michael's interest in even the smallest details helped, too, to pass the time. But not to keep her resolutions.

He asked amazing questions and talked to everyone. He was exceedingly impressed with beer on an airplane, though he made clear his doubts about brew in a can. When the flight attendants served food, he made comparisons with Pegeen's cooking—opinions he shared with everyone.

Michael watched everything. When the steward brought earphones for the in-flight movie, he plugged his in where she showed him. "Sure, there's Irish music in these tubes!"

Revived by the food, Cass felt safe grinning at him. She turned his selection dial and watched his face change at the sounds of rock and roll. Before long, the toes of his shoes were tapping. A potential dancer, she thought. If he could jig, he could boogie. It would be fun to teach him.

But someone else could do it, she corrected herself, because Michael wasn't part of her future.

Up front, a flight attendant pulled down a screen.

"Want to sit here so you can watch the movie, Michael?"

"Movie?" He glanced forward at the images flickering across the screen. "Sure, that would be grand."

She settled into the window seat, still warm from his presence, and rejected the unexpected image of settling back into his arms.

She was tired, that was all. The day had been pretty overwhelming, and she still had Kennedy Airport to get through. On top of that, it would be eight-thirty in the evening before they arrived in St. Louis—something like two a.m. in Ireland. Michael didn't seem bothered by the time change, but if she didn't get some sleep, heaven only knew what feelings she'd be fighting next.

Her nose itched. Mmm, too comfortable to move. Maybe wiggle. Uh-uh, made it worse. Had to scratch.

Eyes still closed, she shifted, felt the soft texture of wool under her hand, against her face. Perplexed, she opened her eyes.

A white collar poked out of a blue tweed sweater. A warm weight engulfed her shoulders, and a toasty scent teased her nostrils. So cozy...

Darn. She jerked up, her heartbeat gearing into double time, a warm coil of pleasure making her hands suddenly shaky.

She'd let her guard down and look what happened. She shoved to the opposite side of the seat.

Michael shifted and tucked the arm she'd rejected around himself. In sleep, his face looked even more handsome, if that were possible. Her fingers yearned to test the slight shadow of stubble on his chin.

Instead, she thrust the window screen up, flooding their space with light. She could see land below. They were coming into New York.

Time for Michael to wake up. For an instant, she felt the impulse to slide close to him again, to feel his warmth. To slip into his arms.

Abruptly, she pulled back, shocked at herself, stunned at the heat the idea generated.

As if he'd heard her thoughts, Michael stirred. One eye popped open and focused, deep blue, on her. His mouth tugged into a lopsided smile. Slowly, he uncurled in a luxurious stretch, grinning. Watching her watch him.

Sheer panic made her look away. He was turning her into a cowardly lion, except that she wasn't searching for a wizard, she was traveling with one. Michael was a man with magical powers. A man who made her feel things she didn't want to feel. A man who wasn't what he claimed to be.

Avoiding his amused smile, she occupied herself by combing her hair and applying lip gloss. As soon as the plane stopped at the terminal, she stood. "Let's go, Michael. First, we have to get our luggage and go through customs. Here, carry this." She snapped the package from Aunt Brigid into his arms.

Had she really thought of herself as a cowardly lion? She sounded more like the Wicked Witch of the West. The man had seriously corrupted her hard-won control.

Ahead, people jammed the aisle retrieving hand luggage. She glanced at her watch which, unfortunately, was still on Irish time.

"Ten after four," a man in front offered.

Good. The flight didn't leave until five-forty. She ticked off the things they had to do: get through customs, recheck luggage, find the gate. They had plenty of time.

Inside the International Terminal, the lines stretched before them. Cass read the various signs: International Passengers to the left, U.S. Residents straight ahead, Non-U.S. Residents, right.

She stopped. Non-U.S. residents? The sign directed non-U.S. residents to another area to be screened for passport and health certificate.

"Michael—" she pointed to the sign "—you go that way."

"You mean we have to separate, Cass?"

"Yes. I'll meet you in the baggage area."

She followed the signs, refusing to look back, refusing to wonder at the concern that had filled his face. Ignoring a sudden onset of loneliness.

Meet you in the baggage area. Ill-fated words if ever she'd spoken them. For the umpteenth time in fifteen minutes, she turned full circle scanning the area for Michael's familiar dark hair. Where was he?

On a nearby baggage carousel, suitcases of all sizes began to flop out, and people crowded forward. Shortly, Case spotted her own case, followed by her garment bag. She tugged them off onto a baggage cart.

Where was Michael's bag? Of course, it would be the one that didn't arrive. Probably a *Daoine Sidh* suitcase that disappeared periodically just out of orneriness. The wry thought failed to lighten her spirits.

At last, his vintage bag slid down the conveyor, and she plopped it onto the cart next to her own baggage. Still no sign of Michael. She wheeled the cart in a zigzag pattern, searching for him among the travelers.

Recognizing some of the Irish passengers from their flight, she pushed the cart over to the door where they'd entered. Five minutes passed, but Michael didn't appear.

She needed to get on to customs.

Propelled by the thought, she directed the cart into line at one of the customs counters. Too late, she realized the agent was opening almost every bag.

What if they asked her to open Michael's bag? How would she explain a man's clothing when there was no man? She edged the cart forward and hoisted the luggage onto the counter, her confidence flagging.

"Business or pleasure?" the woman asked.

"I guess you'd call it business. I'm bringing my father's body home. He died in Ireland."

The woman studied Cass's documents, glanced at the luggage, then handed the papers back. "You're okay. Next?"

Cass couldn't believe it. She'd made it through only to find herself right where she'd been before—worrying about Michael and just as uncertain about what to do. Running her fingers through her hair, she anchored a wayward strand.

The clock showed she had less than an hour before her flight departed. Still she stalled, drawing out the time it took to load the luggage back onto the cart while she searched the area. Michael simply wasn't there.

She pulled her shoulders straight. She needed to get going. Michael was an intelligent, resourceful man. He'd demonstrated that often enough. He could figure out what to do. He could certainly look after himself.

Her steps dragged as she pushed the cart to the check-in counter. A steady stream of people swept by, increasing her sense of isolation in the huge airport.

Such feelings were uncalled for, she chastised herself. As much traveling as she'd done, as many airports as she'd been through, she was used to taking care of herself. She didn't need a man with her.

She shoved the suitcases into the slide-through and spoke firmly to the agent. Bags checked, she marched outside and traipsed along the sidewalk searching for the bus sign and the yellow-and-white bus that would take her to the terminal.

The ride was short, and when the driver pulled to a stop at the main entrance, she was glad to hear him call, "TWA Domestic." Michael could certainly manage to get himself there on his own. He had his ticket and boarding pass, and surely he'd ask for directions. Once there, all he had to do was read the video monitors, just as she was doing.

The rows of words and numbers presented an uncomfortable thought. Michael could read...couldn't he? She forced herself to shrug off the concern. Michael wasn't exactly shy. If he couldn't read, he'd ask someone who could, like a security person. The security area overflowed with uniformed agents, all of whom could help.

Relieved, she slid her purse into the scanner and watched its contents appear on the video screen. The ghostly image jarred her. What if Michael were...

invisible? She shivered, her pulse skipping. Suddenly, she needed to sit down.

If Michael were one of the *Daoine Sidh,* then—how did Fiona say the legend went—people who believed in them could see them? No, it was broader than that. They could be seen when they were with those who believed in them.

If Michael couldn't be seen, he couldn't ask for help. Left to his own resources, he might not have enough time to get to the gate before the flight left.

She plunged into the concourse traffic trying to watch for gate numbers in spite of her racing thoughts.

Ahead, she spied her gate and a clock above the check-in desk. After five o'clock. They'd board the flight soon.

Mentally, she shook herself. She was letting her imagination get away with her. Michael was a real person. She didn't make him visible, because she didn't believe the legends. It was all a matter of logic.

Right.

She spun around and hurried up the concourse toward the security area. Maybe he was being questioned at customs because he had no luggage. Maybe he'd slipped through customs unseen and was looking for their flight in the International Terminal.

What if he mistakenly slipped onto an *international* flight? He might end up in St. Laurent or St. Lucia or somewhere where he couldn't communicate, visible or invisible.

She should have him paged. Yes, that was something she could do. She turned back to the check-in counter.

"Sir?" Her voice sounded slightly hysterical. She needed to calm down. "I have a ticket on this flight, and I need to know if my father's casket has been transferred safely, and my traveling companion . . . I can't find him, and—''

"May I see your ticket, miss?" The agent viewed her over the top of his reading glasses.

"Ticket? Oh, yes." She handed him the bundle of papers, which he scrutinized before tapping on his computer. "Would you please page my—"

"Your ticket and boarding pass are fine, Miss Kohlmann. We'll be boarding soon. The casket will be on Flight 457, arriving St. Louis, 8:21, about twenty minutes before you."

"You mean I'm not on the same flight as my father?" What had Mr. Donovan done?

"No, the casket's on a nonstop." He tapped the keys, then added, "That flight's full and overbooked."

"Nonstop. You mean, this one isn't?"

"You'll have a short layover in Philadelphia, but you'll get to St. Louis at 8:39, so that's really not much difference."

Not much difference? Mr. Donovan's misgivings came back to haunt her like a curse. She'd have to board the flight without knowing if her father's casket was safe.

"Can you check if the casket arrived from Aer Lingus?"

"No, ma'am, but I wouldn't worry. The flight doesn't leave till six-twenty. They've got an hour to get it over there."

Locked in indecision, she searched for some kind of reassurance. The blurred patch of colors she stared at came slowly into focus. Horses? Against the far wall, a colorful poster showed a row of stalls filled with horses. *Happy horses,* it said, *at the Sydney H. Coleman Animal-port.* At Kennedy.

Could Michael have gone there? After all the help he'd given her, after all the concern he'd shown, would he run out on her now for the sake of horses? She didn't want to believe that he would.

Dragging her tote strap up her shoulder, she plodded to an empty seat. There was nothing she could do, she thought sadly. She'd have to trust the airlines and herself to get her father home.

Before long, the agent announced boarding and people crowded to the jetbridge door. No point in standing in line until the area cleared. She was too tired, too drained by everything. She waited with a heavy heart until the agent looked at her meaningfully. "Last call for boarding."

Gathering her hand luggage, she walked to the doorway, then turned back, unable to resist one last look.

Sprinting toward her down the concourse came a dark-haired, broad-shouldered figure in a sweater of wonderful blue. Her heartbeat skyrocketed. "Michael!"

The agent urged her on, so she inched into the jetbridge, walking sideways to see that Michael followed. At the plane's door, the steward hustled them to their seats. Moments later, the plane sliced through strands of yellowish clouds, the city skyscrapers thrusting up from below.

Michael leaned close to the window. "What are those marvelous structures, Cass?" Though he was short of breath, his voice was filled with awe.

"Michael?" She hesitated, struggling for composure. "I was worried. I thought you were going to meet me..."

"I went to see about your father, Cass. I knew you'd be worrying, especially since he's traveling on a different airplane."

"You know? You checked? How could you..."

"I saw him delivered to the plane, but in the end there wasn't time enough to see him put on and get back to you. But, Cass," he said gently, his hand stealing to her forearm in a gesture of comfort, "I'm sure your father's fine. Just think how well things have gone so far...almost as if a good fairy watched over him. 'Tis because he died in Ireland, you know. You've got to believe everything is all right."

Believe. There was that word again. As if believing could make things true. Michael thought so. But everything she'd been taught—by her father, by her grandparents, by her schooling—said believing wasn't enough. She couldn't make a row of numbers add up just by believing. Only her mother had thought otherwise. Only her mother had believed.

"'Twas good that you waited to get on the airplane, Cass, or I might not have found the right one." Michael's soft-spoken brogue wrapped around her, enveloping her in solace, in a sense of well-being that felt very much like happiness.

His hand etched warmth on her arm, and his face, no more than inches from hers, altered from caring to something more intense, something more urgent.

"Michael, why did you go without telling me?" she murmured. She wanted to touch him. She wanted to get lost in his deep blue gaze. Faintly, her Kohlmann training warned, "Caution, Cathleen," but the words faded as he searched her face.

His eyes stalled at her mouth. The distance between them closed, and a new heat swept through her, engulfed her, leaving her incapable of pulling away. As if drawn by some invisible force, she leaned toward him. His breath caressed her cheek, traced a path to her lips, sent a ribbon of desire curling through her. She closed her eyes and reached for him, her hands moving beyond her control until her palms splayed across his chest and her lips touched his—touched magic.

His mouth on hers made flowers bloom, made music soar, flames ignite. Her hands savored the soft texture of his sweater until she encountered the coolness of his neck, a sensation that made her flash with heat and sent her fingers combing into the soft luxury of his hair.

He cast a spell with his mouth, nipping, pressing, mesmerizing her with his fervent gentleness. His hands wove illusions, sliding up her arms to capture her face as if he feared she were a fantasy herself and would slip through his fingers and fly away. He was a magician making her yield, a conjurer stealing her strength, a sorcerer filling her with wildfire.

She kissed him back...she couldn't help herself. Molding to his mouth, opening to his tender probing, tasting his sweet moistness until she heard a longing murmur of desire and knew that it had come from her.

It was the sound that finally slowed her. A familiar sound, the yearnings of an adolescent crush, longing for a man said not to exist. It had all but broken her heart.

She couldn't go through it again.

Suddenly, his hands no longer captured, his lips no longer entreated. She opened her eyes to find him looking down at her fingers where he held them, the tips barely clasped in his.

"Your father will be all right, Cass. I'll stay with you until he's laid to rest." He looked up at her, his face a mask except for a brief flicker of regret. Then he eased into the familiar crooked smile. "After that, maybe you can help me find those Clydesdales."

The impact was like an icy north wind. Michael had pulled away. He'd closed a door...even before she could.

She should be grateful that he'd put a stop to things. He was making it abundantly clear that they were of the same mind. Once her father was safely buried, their . . . association would come to an end.

Chapter Six

Michael followed Cass into the St. Louis airport carrying their hand luggage, a minor load compared to the weight he bore from their fevered encounter on the plane. Cass had yielded, she'd come to him, she'd seemed as desirous as he. But she'd stopped. Frozen. As if the breathless plea that had escaped her lips had scared her away. Like a filly who'd been spooked and shied from shadows.

Had she come then to fear her own feelings?

Without knowing, he'd reached through her defenses, drawn her into passion. He'd frightened her with wanting, and sent her fleeing. In his eagerness to win her, he'd kissed her away. Now he had to convince her not to abandon him altogether. That would be the hardest thing he'd ever done.

Cass strode away, and he heard her murmur, "Blake."

Blake? Was this another word like "taxi"? He shifted the bags and searched the area, seeking an explanation.

"Cathleen." A slender blond man approached, took her hand and leaned to kiss her lightly on the cheek.

Faith, the word *Blake* meant Cass had a suitor. Michael's spirits plummeted.

"Blake, this is Michael O'Shea. Blake Brockman, my boss."

Her boss. Not her suitor. Michael couldn't restrain his relief as he pumped Blake Brockman's hand.

Blake turned back to Cass. "Nice that you met someone on the plane to help you with your things, Cathleen." His private tone excluded Michael. "Let's get your luggage."

Cass hesitated. "I was expecting Jenn to meet me."

"Your friend called me. Something about car trouble and a soccer game. She asked if I might meet your flight."

A frown rippled across Cass's face, a reaction that increased Michael's relief. Blake Brockman wasn't so much a part of her life that he was expected at the airport. Nor did she look at him with love in her eyes.

"If only we hadn't been held up in Philadelphia. I'm afraid to think what's happened to my father."

"Cathleen, your friend checked with the funeral home. They were to pick up the casket as soon as it arrived." Blake cupped her elbow. "You must be exhausted. Come along. I'll take you home."

Cass straightened noticeably and brushed a strand of hair back, a flash of steel in her eyes that Michael welcomed.

"I'm fine, Blake. I'm not leaving till I check on my father. Michael's here to help."

Blake turned to look at Michael more closely. "Do you live in St. Louis, Mr...? Sorry, I've forgotten your name."

"O'Shea. Michael Padraig Brendan O'Shea, from Ireland." He drew the words out with the fullness of his brogue.

"I see," Blake said. "Well, come along, then." He directed them down the deserted concourse.

Over the top of Cass's head, Michael took measure of the man who was her boss but acted more like her keeper. Blake wore a suit the color of storm clouds, appropriate, sure, since he'd shown up like bad weather. Hot weather, from the feel of it, yet Blake looked cool...and uncomfortable. His clothes must have cost a great deal. He likely drove a big car as well, like the one that had crippled the Donovans' truck. Michael breathed in slowly. Did American men wear scents?

Compared with her fancy boss, what would Cass think of himself, Michael wondered. He wore clothes far better suited for work and far more comfortable, though growing warmer by the minute. A bit rumpled, too, but Pegeen always said a confident man needn't be vain. Wouldn't Cass prefer a man at ease with the world to a man who left the scent of flowers in the air?

Still, in spite of Blake's shortcomings, Case didn't seem inclined to send the man away. With Blake around, how was Michael to convince her to take him home with her? By the grace of St. Paddy, an idea had better come to him soon.

Cass rushed ahead of the men to the escalator. Glancing back, she was struck, as always, by Blake's fine-featured face. Like a fashion model, he was almost too good-looking. What a shock to find him there at the airport.

Jenn was up to her tricks again, playing matchmaker at the slightest opportunity. She'd probably called the office and asked for the third partner of Barnsworth, Singley and Brockman as if she were used to calling the Oval Office on alternate days.

Whatever Jenn's motives, Cass wasn't acting very graciously. "Thanks for meeting the plane, Blake."

"No problem, Cathleen. I came from the office."

She might have known he'd be working late, even on a Friday night. "I hope I'm not too far behind on the Jones return," she said. Corporate tax returns were unbearably boring, and she'd planned to be done with this one by now.

"I put someone else on it when you left. You can review it Monday morning."

Efficient, logical, in control. What a relief to come home to Blake after the last few days. As soon as her father was buried, she'd be back to good judgment fulltime.

She turned to glance at Michael. What a contrast to Blake's smooth image. Michael looked rugged, outdoorsy, ready any minute for mischief... or seduction.

The memory set her walking even faster, away from the differences between the two men, the assurances of good sense and the temptations of non-sense, the real world next to an Irish fantasy. The heat—when she looked at Michael.

"It's awfully warm, Blake. What *is* the temperature?"

"The high today was ninety-nine. A record, I think."

The dreadful fact reminded her of her father's state, propelling her into a jog all the way to the ticket counter.

"Kohlmann," she said to the agent. "My father was supposed to be on flight 457. I need to find out if he arrived."

"Miss Kohlmann, no one's been through in over an hour. Was your father being assisted to travel?"

She flinched at her abruptness. "I'm sorry, I mean my father's *casket*. Schmidt Funeral Home was supposed to pick it up." She pushed her papers toward him.

He clamped a phone between his ear and shoulder while he shuffled through her papers. "No answer in cargo. But I'm sure your father's casket's been picked up."

Blake stepped forward. "I'll take you home, Cathleen."

"I can't leave until I know my father's been picked up."

"Cathleen . . . ?"

The concern on Blake's face made her pause. "Blake, this man doesn't even know for sure if the casket arrived."

Alarmed at her own words, she turned back to the agent. "Sir, I have to know for sure. If you won't direct me to the cargo area, I'll find it myself. Come on, Michael."

"Wait." The agent hesitated. "Okay, I'll take you."

He beckoned someone to take his place, then led them down the escalator and through the concourse to an unmarked door. He unlocked the door and pulled it open.

They stepped out into the heat emanating from the dark tarmac below and followed the agent down metal stairs to a large door. The door slid up, releasing a welcome stream of cool air.

Inside, the white light of fluorescent tubes revealed boxes and crates casting angular shadows. A flaking metal desk sat off to one side. The door slid closed behind them.

"Jake?" the agent called. "Jake, you still here?"

"Yeah?" a far-off voice answered from the cavernous warehouse. "Who's 'at?" A man in a soiled khaki jumpsuit appeared. "Hey, man. Whaddaya doin' down in the inferno?" He stared at Cass's red hair.

She stepped forward. "I'm Cass Kohlmann. I sent a casket on flight 457 from Kennedy tonight. Has it arrived?"

"Hey, yeah, lady. We got two caskets tonight. Real unusual. One's been picked up. The other one's right over there." He pointed toward a shadowy corner, and Cass hurried over.

"The hearse come by for the first one, like about nine-thirty. Le'see, where's them papers?"

"Look, Michael." Relief brought tears to her eyes. She pointed to the word KOLAM stenciled on the crate. "Dad's been picked up. Thank God."

She smiled at Jake. "I can't tell you how relieved I am. Now we'll get out of here and give you some peace."

They turned just as a horn sounded outside and the door swung up. A black hearse had backed up to the doorway.

"Schmidt Funeral Home," said the driver. "I got papers for a casket. Kohlmann?"

Cass's heart wrenched.

"Kolam," the worker corrected. "Hey, back that rig in. You're lettin' all the air out, man."

"Come on, Cathleen, let's slip out before he closes the door." Blake attempted to guide her forward.

"Wait. He said 'Kohlmann,' and Schmidt's the funeral home I contacted."

"Are you sure you didn't misunderstand?" Blake sounded on the brink of impatience.

"Another minute to find out won't be a great loss, will it now?" Michael asked, stepping nearer.

"Here's the papers." The driver held them out.

"Yeah, 'Kolam,'" the worker answered. "Right over here." He'd led the driver to the box in the corner.

"Nah. The papers say 'Kohlmann.' Supposed to be on TWA 457. All the way from Ireland."

Cass couldn't keep quiet. "Jake, what about the other casket? Who picked it up?"

The man examined the papers, then rubbed his whiskered chin. "Let's see. Them other papers…" He traipsed to the metal desk where he leafed through papers on a clipboard. "Where the. . . ." he muttered.

"Are you *sure* the other box had Kohlmann written on it?" Cass asked.

"Yeah, sure." He paused. "I think so. I know they both started with a K." He avoided looking at her.

"Do you remember the name of the funeral home that came for the other casket? Please, try to remember. Jake, my father's in that casket. I'm bringing him home to be buried beside my mother. You've got to remember who picked him up."

"Lady, I can't find them papers, and I'm gonna catch hell from my supervisor. Maybe even lose my job. I don't remember the name of the funeral home. Maybe it was Kutis—or Kriegshauser. Maybe that was the K I was thinkin' of. Them two names sound awful lot alike." He looked miserable.

"Okay." She fought to keep defeat from her voice. "Please, just find out. And call me as soon as you do, no matter what time." She handed him her card and turned toward the door. "Take me home, Michael." Hearing her own words, she stopped. Damn.

She squared her shoulders, drew in a deep breath. "I mean, Blake, would you please take me home."

* * *

With the help of St. Paddy, Michael would not let Cass get away. He carried their luggage, a sizable load to be sure, enough so that he could drag his feet without suspicion. He had to come up with an idea.

Blake walked ahead briskly. "My car's out this door."

"Mmm," Cass murmured.

She was obviously exhausted. If Michael had his way, he'd see her sleeping soon.

Blake led them into the steamy underground garage. "I offered to direct Mr. O'Shea, Cathleen, but he insists he's going to your place. I'll have to hear from you on that."

"Cass, I'll not leave you to deal with this alone. I intend to help find your father."

She didn't respond.

Michael looked at her with new concern. If he didn't convince her now, he'd be alone, and invisible, in St. Louis of America. He'd be disqualified from the race.

Blake stopped beside a car with the word Porsche stretched across the back, and Michael's worries multiplied. The car was much too small for three people.

"I wasn't expecting two." Blake sounded a bit defensive. He unlocked the passenger door. "Get in, Cathleen. I'll just point Mr. O'Shea toward the cabs." He opened the front hood. "If you'll give me those bags, Mr. O'Shea."

"Cass?" Michael said, trying to balance persuasion and insistence in his voice.

For the first time since they'd left the cargo area, Cass showed signs of life. Her gray eyes glinted. "Put everything in the trunk, Blake. Please," she added more softly. "Michael can sit in the passenger seat."

Sure, St. Paddy was smiling on Michael tonight. He slung the bags into the trunk, glad to hide his elation.

"But, Cathleen," Blake asked, "how will you get home?"

"You're taking me, Blake. I'll sit on Michael's lap."

Stay awake, Cass commanded herself. Despite the crackle of tension in Blake's small car, she fought her exhaustion. She had to stay awake. She had to figure out how to find her father.

As if anyone could possibly sleep in the electrical storm brewing between Michael and Blake. Blake sat ramrod-straight in the driver's seat, and Michael, instead of trying to ease the situation, sat hunkered down, his arms circled around her like an enveloping nest.

As if anyone could possibly sleep in the position she was in. Being so close to Michael made her warmer than the air conditioner could ever help, made her strain to sit with the least amount of body contact. Because contact with Michael brought back memories she needed to forget.

The more she held herself away from him, the more her muscles ached. She longed to fold herself against him. When she began to tremble, she had to give in, to let herself relax and curl against his chest. Slowly, her head came to rest in the curve of his shoulder.

He felt so good. He smelled of Irish air and masculinity—and just the faintest hint of soap.

"Cass. Wake up. You're home."

Whack—her head thumped the ceiling of the car. Reaching up to touch the throbbing spot, she pulled herself away from Michael's arms. She suddenly felt cool where before she'd been warm against him. And she felt something more—regret.

Blake opened the car door that had braced her, letting her slip backward until Michael's strong arm tightened around her again. She didn't want to move.

"Give me your hand, Cathleen," Blake instructed.

"Easy, Cass, take it slow." Michael shifted to help her turn. She could feel the muscles of his thighs as he moved, feel the strength of his arms as he guided her. He handed her to Blake who helped her out, and she felt as if she'd been cast adrift.

"Trunk's open, Mr. O'Shea. I'll help Cathleen." Blake wrapped his arm around her waist, and she waited for the warm glow to resume. It didn't.

At her door, Blake took her key just as Michael bounded up the stairs with the luggage.

Blake unlocked the door and pushed it open. "My God, the heat is ghastly in there." He moved to the threshold. "Where's the light? I'll get your air conditioner going and—"

"Blake, you've been wonderful, but I can manage now." She stepped in front of him. "It's late and I'm sure you have golf in the morning." She motioned for Michael to slip in behind her. "Really, I'll be fine." She backed into the apartment, easing the door shut. "Thanks for picking me up." She smiled through the six-inch crack, then closed the door with a click to cut off the sound of her conscience.

In the close darkness, she leaned back against the wall and let out a long breath. She'd made it home at last.

But her father hadn't. The thought shook her as if she'd slammed the door. She needed to find her father.

"Cass, could we have a light? I don't want to step on the cat."

She could sense Michael moving nearby. She flipped the switch just as his hand brushed her shoulder. His touch was warm, like the aura he'd exuded in the car.

She shouldn't have let him come home with her.

Sidestepping his touch, she hurried to the hall, adjusted the air conditioner and tugged sheets and towels from the closet.

"Here, Michael." She plopped the linens into his arms and pointed to the back bedroom, indicating the bathroom on the way. "You shower first." She retreated quickly to her room, a safe distance away. "I'll see you in the morning."

Michael surveyed the room, the quilt-covered bed and the dressing table with photos framing the mirror, then set his bag and linens down and turned back to the door.

He intended to see Cass tucked in and sleeping. With him right beside her would be his preference. He still felt the softness of her body from the ride in Blake Brockman's car. But he knew such a sleeping arrangement wasn't likely.

Slipping off his shoes, he padded to the living room in his stocking feet, feeling the sand-colored carpet yield to his tread. No time to marvel at such wonders now. Cass needed his care.

"...a casket shipped from Ireland. This evening, about nine-thirty. Kohlmann, with a K. Are you sure?" She sat at a small white-topped table in the kitchen, her feet curled under her. A purple robe hugged her soft curves.

"Thanks." She replaced the receiver with a sigh and made a mark on the yellow page of a large book.

"What is it you're doing, Cass?"

Her hand flew to her heart. "You startled me. I thought you were going to shower."

"I came to help, remember? You should be in bed."

Her gaze flew to him. Her bare feet slid to the floor, and she sat up straighter, brushing fingers back through her hair. "I'm calling funeral homes."

"There cannot be funeral homes open at this hour."

"I've talked to a few people."

She sounded defensive and defeated—he hated to hear that. Quickly, he slid the book across the table. "Tell me what to do. I'll call—you shower." She eyed him dubiously.

"I'm bigger than you, in case you'd be wanting to fight."

She sighed again. "Just call the next number." She demonstrated, punching lighted buttons on the equipment. Each one responded with a musical beep.

He pointed Cass out of the kitchen with an exaggerated scowl. Following her example, he punched in the numbers and listened to a series of buzzes. No one talked.

Out of the corner of his eye, he caught a flash of purple. Cass had curled into a chair in the living room.

Suddenly, a man said, "Hello?"

Michael stiffened. "Hello? This is Michael O'Shea. Hello...? Are you there?" He heard a click that sent a stab of alarm racing through him. The man hadn't heard his voice. What did that mean?

Cass covered the distance to his side before he could return the instrument to its cradle. "Did you get someone?"

At least *she* could still hear him, could still see him. "Just talking to myself."

"Talking to yourself is a bad sign."

"Cass, I know you're tired, even if you won't admit it. It's pointless to call anymore tonight."

Her eyes turned pewter like a misty morning in Glinbrendan. He longed to take her in his arms, to comfort her. She looked at him for a long time, and he thought he saw her sadness reach out to him, a sadness that wrung his heart. He shoved the chair back and took her hands.

Her gaze faltered, then swept down to where he held her so carefully. She pulled away, sliding her hands into her pockets. "We'll call again in the morning."

Faith, there were those walls again. He dared not press her, couldn't risk her rejection. Best only to offer the soothing of words. "Sure, tomorrow we'll find your father, Cass."

Without answering, she walked to her bedroom and closed the door.

Cass stood inside her room, her fists plunged deep into her pockets, her heart pounding. She'd almost reached out to Michael. Standing so close to him, seeing his face so full of concern, for a moment she'd let herself feel the grief. And the wanting. She'd wanted his comfort, wanted him to hold her. She'd only barely managed to stop herself. His withdrawal on the plane had hurt, more than she could admit, and she wouldn't let that happen again.

She began to empty her suitcase, her mind churning all the while. She'd made a total mess of things. Ms. Logical CPA had done everything wrong.

She just couldn't stay away from that fairy ring, could she? Had to stir up all the old questions about Michael, and now he practically lived in her pocket. Made her want things she shouldn't.

Worse than that, she'd insisted on dragging her father back to St. Louis, and now he was lost. She had to find him, but how?

The walls of the room closed in. Abandoning her unpacking, she stole out to the now-darkened living room. Pacing, she fought the tightness in her throat.

Had she been wrong to want her father in St. Louis? She hadn't thought so when she'd made the decision. It had seemed right to want her parents to be buried together.

A shiver ran down her back. She dropped onto the sofa and slid into a corner, hugging a plump pillow. Tears brimmed in her eyes.

She'd lost her father long ago because she'd followed the impulses of her feelings, because she'd ignored the straight thinking he personified. Now she'd lost him again.

Slowly, she let herself feel the loneliness she'd buried so many years ago, the sadness she'd not allowed to surface even when she'd learned of her father's death. The tears broke free and flowed, releasing the grief, letting go the hurt. She mourned the losses, acknowledged the pain.

When Michael's arm slid around her in the darkness, drawing her into his warmth, she didn't resist.

"Sure, Cass, 'tis a good thing to cry." His quiet brogue wrapped her in comfort.

"Oh, Michael, maybe I was wrong." She couldn't stop the words, nor the tears. "I wanted Mom and Dad to be together, but it's created so many problems. Really, bringing Dad back here was more for me." Her voice caught.

"There's no wrong in wanting those you love near, Cass."

"But having them together doesn't matter anymore. They'll never know. Mom and Dad are...dead." She struggled to say the word, her voice ragged and harsh.

Without loosening his embrace, Michael tugged a handkerchief from his pocket and handed it to her. She pressed it to her mouth to muffle the sobs.

He held her gently, rocking her in a soothing rhythm.

Finally, she found her voice. "There were so many things Dad and I should have talked about." She wiped tears from her cheeks. "But now it's too late. I should never have let my emotions get involved. That's why he's lost."

"Cass, a decision made with love is never wrong." His velvet voice soothed her. "There's an old Irish saying, 'Never was one door shut but another was opened.' You'll see. Tomorrow we'll find that door. You've got to believe."

Believe. Believe. Believe. With his rocking, the word became a mantra. Slowly, she let her body yield to the warmth and comfort he offered. The front of his shirt where she laid her hand was wet with her tears. The chin resting against her forehead prickled her skin with its stubble. She could hear the drumming of his heart, and her heart, fast and loud. She knew that if she looked up, he would kiss her, and his kiss would taste of sunshine and green pastures and misty hollows. And she was glad she was too tired to move. She was glad he didn't lift her chin. Because she knew she would succumb to his persuasion. She would kiss him back, deeply and wholly. She would believe.

Bright sunlight filtered in from behind the ivory-colored drapes. The smell of bacon and strong coffee hung in the air. Cass's eyes flew open and she realized she was in her bed.

Suddenly, memories of last evening filled her with embarrassment. Shocked, she sat up. She'd cried . . . in front of Michael. Worse than that, she'd talked. Told him much too much. And he'd comforted her. In a way that had made her want his kiss. To want more than his kiss.

She must have fallen asleep in his arms, and he'd carried her to her room. To her bed.

Thank goodness her robe was still wrapped around her. Michael was too much a gentleman to take advantage of... a situation. She couldn't blame him completely for the closeness they'd shared. She hadn't exactly pushed him away. Heat warmed her cheeks and spread through her body. She had to get over feeling this way.

Clanging pans snapped her back to the present. She wasn't ready to face him, yet she could only guess what Michael was doing to her kitchen. Swinging out of bed, she hurried to the bathroom.

The image in the mirror made her turn the cold water on full blast. Holding a cold washcloth to her swollen eyes, she prayed for a miracle. Not even a miracle would repair that much damage, she admitted. The way she looked would just have to do.

She walked quietly to the kitchen doorway and tried to assess the damage Michael's noise had threatened.

"Morning, Cass." He smiled, his eyes as bright blue as the morning sky. His dark hair glistened with moisture, the waves partially subdued. He wore tan trousers and a white shirt, the sleeves folded to midarm, the neck open to wisps of dark curly hair. He'd forgotten to put on his shoes. How could he look so good so early?

"Have a seat. I've just about everything ready." On the table sat a plastic glass holding three bright red geraniums. She recognized them from the pots that flanked the entry door downstairs. Her landlady would have a fit.

She should be having a fit. She should be busy trying to locate her father, not standing there appraising Michael.

She'd let him come with her for only one reason. He was here to help find her father—she needed to remember that.

After that, Michael was history.

Chapter Seven

The phone rang. Michael stared at the white instrument on the kitchen counter. In the distance, he could hear the steady splash of the shower.

If it rang again, he'd have to answer. It might be the man from the airport, the call Cass waited for so anxiously.

It rang once more. He hesitated, then picked it up. "Hello?"

"Hello?" A woman's voice inquired.

"Hello. This is the home of Cathleen Kohlmann." Michael said the words slowly and clearly.

"Hello? Cass?" A pause. "I don't know." The voice diminished. "Someone picked it up, but no one's answering."

Michael heard a click. Reluctantly, he put the phone back in the cradle. Abruptly, it rang again. He snatched it up.

"Hello. I'm here. Can you hear me?"

"Cass? This is Adam. Are you there?" The man's voice rose with concern.

"Adam, don't hang up. I'll go get—" Another click.

Uneasily, Michael replaced the receiver, aware of what his unheard voice might mean—that what he'd tried so hard to prevent could be happening—Cass's belief in him might be fading.

Faith, he had no one to blame but himself. He shouldn't have held her so close last night, shouldn't have comforted her so lovingly. But she'd looked so alone, she'd felt so small and smelled of sweet salt tears and warm moist skin. When he'd taken her in his arms, she'd responded almost with relief, her soft body molding into the planes of his own. By the faith of St. Paddy, it had taken all his will to keep from kissing her. He'd had to be very stern with himself when he'd carried her to her bed, because his desire to comfort had changed to the pure flames of desire.

Most likely, she'd been put off by his interference, by his very presence. She grieved Wil's loss with no feelings left for anything else, at least none that she'd let herself feel. After their kiss on the airplane, she might even have wished him away.

For a moment, he let his mind drift to Glinbrendan. He hoped the O'Sheas were thinking of him for he was in need of a miracle. As soon as he helped Cass find her father, she'd be sending him packing. He had to find a way to make her love him—and that surely would take a miracle.

"Okay, Michael. Let's get busy."

At the sight of Cass, he felt himself respond again, and he knew he'd have to turn up his guard. She wore a narrow white skirt revealing slender legs up to her knees and a white shirt that molded softly to the curves of her breasts. A small red figure over her heart looked like a person on a horse. Faith, the woman was a temptation.

He pulled out her chair, focusing on the damp curls of her hair. "I'll read the numbers. You do the talking."

"I want to call the airport first."

Several tries later, she gave up. "No one answered at the cargo area." She glanced anxiously at the clock above the stove. "We'd better try the funeral homes."

She took up where he'd left off the night before, but each contact deepened the gray of her eyes. No one had heard of Willem Kohlmann. No one had a casket in error.

Cass tugged fingers through her hair, unaware of the windswept look it gave her. Worry tensed her mouth.

"What can I do? What if we don't find my father anywhere? What if his casket never made it here?"

"Cass, the man at the airport said—"

The phone rang, and they both jumped.

Cass grabbed it. "Hello? Oh. Blake."

Michael walked away, but he couldn't resist listening.

"I'm doing okay. I'm phoning. Michael's helping."

Michael turned in time to see her frown.

"Tomorrow? But Blake, we haven't found my father yet—"

His spirits lifted at her use of the word *we*.

"You want me to bring Michael?" She paused to look at him. "That's considerate of you, Blake—" her voice softened "—but he won't be here much longer."

A pause. Michael refused to look at her, pretending not to have heard, ignoring the sharp dejection that hit.

"If we locate my father's casket— Wait, there's another call on my line. I'll let you know, Blake."

Another call? Michael roused himself from his plunging spirits.

"Hello?" Her face brightened. "Michael, it's the man from the airport. Oh, no!" She scribbled on a scrap of paper. "I have it." She clapped the receiver down.

"Come on, Michael. We're going to find my father."

Shoes in hand, Michael followed her out the kitchen door only to halt with a gasp. Faith, the heat felt like the blacksmith's shed in Glinbrendan.

He hopped down the wooden stairs trying to pull his shoes on at the same time. At the bottom of the steps, a wide panel in the side of the building slowly ascended revealing a small blue car. The engine roared, and the car screeched out of the building, sliding to a halt beside him. The door on the right popped open.

He jumped in and held on tight. The tires squalled when Cass pulled onto a tree-lined road and whipped the car around the vehicles ahead. He muttered an oath and wiped his forehead, already damp with perspiration. "If you don't slow down, they'll be burying us along with your father."

The car raced onto a highway.

"They're burying my father in the wrong place, Michael. The man at the airport found the papers and called the funeral home. They said the Kohlmann casket was to be buried this morning—but it's in the wrong cemetery. We have to stop them."

"We're going to stop a funeral, Cass?" Could such things happen in America?

She swung the car off the main road. Stopping at a red light, she studied a scrap of paper, then turned left and stomped on the accelerator.

Almost immediately, a wailing sound filled Michael's ears.

"Oh, no!"

"What is it?"

The sound increased, and a car with flashing lights pulled up behind them, the whine rising and falling. Cass steered to the side of the road.

"Let me do the talking, Michael."

A man in a uniform approached. Michael's muscles tensed, and he fumbled with the door latch. If they were in danger, he had to be ready to act.

Cass's window slid down.

"Going to a fire, miss? You ran a light and hit thirty-five in about five seconds flat ... in a twenty-five zone. Driver's license?"

Cass handed him a small card. "I'll pay the ticket, but, please, I need your help."

Sliding his dark glasses down, the uniformed man listened while she explained.

"Okay, miss. Follow me."

The car pulled out, its lights still flashing, its siren rising from the brief reprieve of silence.

Cass followed until he turned in to a driveway flanked by a wrought-iron gateway with the word Rosemont entwined in metal flowers overhead. Beyond, headstones shaded by overhanging trees traced a restful pattern across the lawn.

"There, Cass." Michael directed her toward a mound of dirt to the right. He noticed another car enter the cemetery behind them followed by a long black vehicle. Shortly, a white car joined the procession.

She stopped near the grave site, and her face paled. "I don't see the casket." She shot out of the car leaving Michael struggling to open his door.

He jackknifed out, flinching at the stifling air. Ahead, Cass ran toward the open grave.

"Please, wait," she shouted to the two men standing on either side. In the opening, just below ground, a simple casket descended, lowered on wide canvas straps. "That's the casket from Donovan's. Please don't bury my father."

Their gazes shifted from Cass to Michael and came to rest on the man in uniform behind. They stopped the machine.

"We got orders to bury this casket, sir," the smaller man said. "There wasn't no funeral, 'cause the guy—I mean the deceased—came from outta town, see. New York, I think."

Cass stepped forward. "You're burying the wrong casket. I mean, this is my father's casket from Ireland."

"Look, lady, I don't know nothin'—"

"Miss Kohlmann?" Three men approached from behind. "We're from the funeral homes," the leader said. "The airport notified us of this unfortunate mix up. I'm afraid this has been a serious mistake, but nothing that can't be rectified."

The men produced documents, and they gathered Cass into a huddle. Michael walked away, leaving her to deal with them alone. He wouldn't interfere. She was handling the error much better than he would, and he was confident she'd finish her mission without any more help from him.

He strolled to the end of the grave where he thought Wil's head might rest and looked down on the modest casket. "'Tis quite a lass you have for a daughter, Wil Kohlmann. You can be proud of her. She loves you every bit as much as you loved her. Truly, she grieves the differences that lay between you, just as you did."

He glanced at Cass, still deep in conference with the others. "She's why you're here, my friend. I'm hoping you're not minding the heat too much. If you'll be patient a bit longer, she'll soon have you resting cool and comfortable, next to your very own Molly O'Neil. Because your daughter loves you."

Michael glanced up to be sure he could still see Cass. Though she stood with the men, she stared at him, a puzzled expression on her face. Had she noticed him talking?

He ambled away a few yards and surveyed the cemetery, ignoring her probing gaze. Finally, she turned away.

Michael directed his thoughts upward to the towering trees. "Your daughter is a hardheaded one, friend Wil, near as much as you, I'd wager. But if by chance—if there truly be luck of the Irish—should she one day learn to love me, would you give your blessing?"

The sound of squeaking interrupted his reverie. The men had reversed the machine and were slowly raising the casket. An understanding had been reached.

His gaze flew to find Cass. She was standing just on the far side of the grave. Tears glinted in her eyes.

Stunned, Michael stared at her. Had she heard? Did she know that she'd stolen his heart? If she heard him ask Wil for her hand, she'd know he'd fallen in love with her. If so, would she turn away?

"Mr. O'Shea, would you give us some help?" one of the men from the funeral home asked.

Thankful for the reprieve from the turmoil of his feelings, he helped them carry the casket to the hearse.

"We'll take care of everything, Miss Kohlmann." The man mopped his forehead with a handkerchief. "Meet us at Green Oaks, and we'll lay your father to rest right away."

Everyone shook hands. Michael watched as the car with the flashing lights led the hearse and the other vehicles along the narrow road out of the cemetery.

"Come on, Michael," Cass said. "I'm afraid to let my father out of sight. I won't let him get lost again."

Before she could open the car door, he turned her gently to face him. Unable to stop himself, he risked holding her shoulders, offering at least that small touch of comfort. He looked down at her, drawn by the cloudy gray of her eyes, the tears still clinging to her thick lashes. He had never seen her look so sad.

"Cass, your father will be fine. You mustn't let yourself feel so bad for the adventures he's had. Knowing Wil, I'd wager he's chuckling this very minute, hoping for one more mishap before he settles down for good."

Light flashed from her gray eyes like sparks from struck steel. "You *knew* my father." She pulled away from him. "Why didn't you tell me?"

Saints in heaven, he'd done it now, for sure. He reached to catch her hands.

She sidestepped, then halted.

Michael heard it, too. A telephone in the middle of a cemetery? What kind of sorcery was this?

The tone broke the stillness again. Her car phone!

"Don't move, Michael. Don't you dare disappear again. I want the truth about my father." Cass jerked the car door open and snatched up the instrument.

"Hello? Oh, Jenn." She turned to watch Michael. Hard as it was to concentrate on Jenn's barrage of words, she would not take her eyes off him.

Jenn paused. "Cass, you sound funny. Are you okay?"

"Yes, really. Thanks for the invitation. It would be good to see you and Adam. Can we just leave it open?"

"We? Cass, who's with you?"

"Remember when my dad shipped me to Ireland and I met that...person?"

"The handsome Irish lad," Jenn said, mimicking a brogue. "The one you got in so much trouble over? He's with you? Cass, now you've got to come. I can't wait to see him."

"He's got some explaining to do, first, if he doesn't disappear." She saw Michael wince.

"Come on, Michael." She replaced the phone and started the engine while he sandwiched his solid frame into the car.

Fearful of what he might tell her, Cass focused on her driving, holding back questions, her speculations tumbling one over another.

Her father could only have known Michael if he were real, because Wil Kohlmann didn't believe in anything imaginary. So what Michael was about to tell her had to be the proof she'd sought, proof that he truly existed, that her imagination hadn't gone haywire.

And if her father had known Michael, he must have accepted that she was rational. Suddenly, she wanted more than anything for Michael and her father to have known each other. But she'd have to be on guard. She had to be sure he spoke the truth.

She negotiated a turn onto the highway. "All right, Michael. You've been calling my father 'Wil' ever since Ireland. You've been talking about him like you were good old buddies. How could you have known him?"

"It's time you heard the story, Cass. I've been wanting to tell you." He almost said, "...about the father you didn't know," but something held him back. This wasn't the time yet for her to hear everything. He'd tell her how they'd met, but he'd wait to tell her the rest. She wasn't ready to accept her father as a believer. She wasn't yet ready to accept herself.

Cass straightened. "How did you meet my father?"

He shifted so he could watch her face, making sure his arm across the back of the seat didn't threaten her. "The last year or so, your father came often from Cork. Weekends and holidays, and the length of his summer vacation."

He remembered the first time he saw blocky Wil Kohlmann with Cass's Uncle Kevin. Michael knew him immediately as the father of the lass he'd taken to Glinbrendan the day of the storm, the lass who'd left Ireland with his heart. Perhaps he could learn if she'd be back.

"Your uncle brought your father to the stables when he had work to do. Your father was interested in the horses."

Wil wandered around the stables so much that Michael worried he wouldn't be able to work. Rather than hide his activities, he decided to make himself known. He stole Wil's cap, snatched it right off his head like a gust of wind, and dangled it up on the weather vane. Then he sat on a bale of hay and watched Uncle Kevin climb up on the roof to retrieve it, then cap in hand, climb down and proceed to tell Wil the story of the Daoine Sidh. Kevin bragged of the deeds of Pegeen O'Shea and the healing hands of Mick, her son.

"Mick O'Shea," Will said. "Is that the Michael O'Shea Cathleen claimed to have met?"

"Aye. Cathleen has her mother's love of the stories," was all Kevin had answered.

"One weekend, when your uncle had extra work, he left your father on his own. Wil had his eye on a maverick named Satan, a fine steed. Your father had a good sense for that.

"He wandered into the stall where I was checking the animal's hooves. He came up careful, for I'd left the stall door open, and he reached out to pat Satan's nose. He was talking real soft—I remember his words as clear. He said, 'Must be Mick O'Shea that's got you so calm today, big fellow.' So I just came 'round and introduced myself."

He relished Cass's look of astonishment, couldn't help but grin, though he quickly sobered. He wanted her to believe the scenes he remembered so vividly.

He'd stepped into view and greeted Wil, then held his breath. Wil frowned. He squinted. He took one cautions step and stared into the semidarkness of the stall. In a voice almost a whisper, he said, "Mick? Mick O'Shea?"

It was all Michael could do to keep from hugging the man. "Aye, sir, Michael O'Shea. Pleased to make your acquaintance, sir," he said, and offered his hand. Slowly, with a hint of fear in his eyes, Wil reached out. Cautiously, they closed hands. Michael felt the strength of Wil's grasp. Then they both roared into laughter. It had seemed as if Wil were as elated as he. It had seemed that they'd both been waiting just to meet.

"My father could see you? I mean, he spoke to you?"

Michael saw the doubt in her eyes. "Your father said, 'You're just as Cathleen described you. I didn't think a man's eyes could be so blue.' "

Cass glanced at him skeptically.

"He told me you called your aunt Brigid 'Biddie.' "

She inhaled audibly and twisted to search his face.

"We went fishing for brown trout, and he taught me how to tie flies. I caught the most with his 'Pink Peeper.' "

"Oh, Michael..." Tears brimmed in her eyes.

"I know, Cass. He said he created it and you named it, when you were still his little girl."

She turned back to the road, fumbling in her purse for a tissue. Michael and her father had been friends. He couldn't have know about the Pink Peeper any other way.

"Why didn't my father tell me," she whispered.

"He planned to, Cass. He was going to invite you for Christmas. But first he wanted to learn to ride. He wanted to show you he'd changed."

Of course. Her mother had loved to ride, but her father had always refused to learn.

"He asked me to teach him to ride, Cass. We always rode together..."

His silence made her turn, and she recognized sadness not unlike her own in his eyes.

"...except that day. I couldn't go with him that day. I'm sorry, Cass," he said quietly. "I might have saved his life."

She saw then his unguarded grief. He was blaming himself for her father's death.

"No." She reached for his hand. "My father's death was an accident. You weren't to blame. You gave him something wonderful. Except for my mother, he never had a friend... like you."

She felt his strong hand grasp hers, and she tightened her own grip. Their eyes met and held, stirring her more than his touch. What she felt went beyond gratitude, beyond friendship. Pulling her hand away, she turned back to the road, her heart pounding.

Appreciation. Sympathy. Relief. She ticked off the feelings she should be experiencing, those, and nothing more. Not longing, not desire for this extraordinary man.

In a very short time, she'd lay her father to rest beside
her mother. What Michael had just told her would let her
put to rest a long-term heartache as well. Then she could
get on with her life with a sense of peace—and whole-
ness.

"'Tis good we arrived in time to rescue your father."

Michael sounded suddenly distant. She shivered, her
flesh nubbing as if a cold wind had brushed her. She
reached to adjust the air conditioner.

At the intersection, she turned the car and watched for
the familiar stone columns that marked the entrance to
Green Oaks Cemetery, named for the tall trees that gave
a parklike atmosphere to the grounds. She searched for
the reddish-purple flowers that usually bloomed in
abundance along the hedgerows. Fuchsia, her father had
told her, her mother's favorite flower. It grew profusely
in Ireland. The flowers were why he'd chosen this place
for her.

Cass drove slowly along the winding route to the plot.
When she reached the hearse, they left her car, and she
led Michael to the small rose quartz headstone that
marked her mother's grave:

Molly Cathleen O'Neil Kohlmann
1943 - 1971
Beloved

Her father's casket was there, too. Cass nodded to the
two men, and they started it on its slow descent into the
plot next to her mother's. Beside her, she heard the soft
lilt of music, Michael's haunting melody shifting from
major to minor key, telling of pleasure and of sorrow.
Michael hummed, his voice deep and rich, like a cello in
the still, bright air.

His hand touched hers, then slipped around it, nesting her in his rough warmth. She didn't pull away. Right now, she needed more than anything to share her grief. Michael had loved her father, too. He grieved, too, with a melody that didn't falter.

When at last his song ceased, he drew her to his side. Scooping up a handful of soil, he threw it into the opening at their feet. *"Slán leat, ma achora.* Goodbye, my friend. God bless."

Cass followed his example, letting the moist earth fall from her hand. Tears slipped from her eyes and she whispered, "Bye, Dad. I love you."

Michael slid his arm around her shoulder. She looked up to find him lost in his own melancholy. Her heart tugged toward him. Suddenly, she wanted to hold him, to comfort him as he had her, to smooth her fingers back through his hair and stroke the strong line of his jaw. A tremor shook her, pulsed against him, and he turned to her, his eyes full of something stronger than grief—full of the reflection of her own wanting.

She pulled away. She had to stop feeling this way. Wanting Michael wasn't part of the life she'd planned. She turned and ran to the car.

Chapter Eight

"Cass, it's about time!" Jenny Johnson threw open the screen door of the old three-story home and flung her arms around Cass. "And you must be Michael." Releasing Cass, Jenn wiped her floury hand on her cutoffs and extended it toward her. "I'm Jenn." She appraised him from head to feet. "Goodness, Michael, you certainly are—"

Cass jabbed an elbow into Jenn's ribs.

"...WEL-come. Yes, you certainly are." Jenn grinned and stared cross-eyed at Cass. "Come on, you two. Adam, Annie, Todd," she hollered into the house. "Cass is here."

Cass exhaled with relief. The madcap Johnsons were just the distraction she needed from the pain of saying goodbye to her father and from her more than disturbing feelings for Michael. The Johnsons put things into perspective.

" 'Scuse the mess,'' Jenn said, leading them through the toy-strewn entryway into the bright family room. The sounds of dusty jazz music and the scent of baking bread floated in the air.

Footsteps thundered, and Todd whooped into the room, blond hair tousled, Band Aids crisscrossing both knees. Annie followed close behind, her brown hair swaying in a ponytail like her mother's.

The children stumbled to a stop, and Annie's mouth dropped. "Are you the leprechaun?" she whispered with awe.

Michael knelt in front of her, his eyes full of pleasure. "You must be Annie."

The girl nodded, unable to recapture her tongue.

"I'm not a leprechaun," he said, "but I am one of the Good People." Flashing Cass a wink, he added, "If *you're* good, I'll tell you all about us."

Now Cass stared. After she'd finally put her doubts to rest, he was confessing to be one of the *Daoine Sidh?* She didn't need this.

"Cass. It's good to see you. We were getting worried," Jenn's husband, Adam, said as he entered the room.

She returned Adam's hug, evading Michael's devilish grin.

"Welcome to our humble abode, Mike. Hope you're not daunted by chaos." Adam shook Michael's hand. "Come on outside. There's a wisp of wind out there, and ribs on the grill."

Michael's smile held, but the mischief faded. He sought Cass's eyes, his own watchful again.

"Wait, Daddy." Annie tugged Adam's fuzzy arm. "I want to hear the story of the Good People."

"Come on, then. I wouldn't mind hearing it myself."
Adam ambled to the kitchen. "I'll grab a couple of
beers."

"Why don't you all come?" Michael looked hard at
Cass.

"Good idea," said Jenn. "I'll get lemonade."

When they'd gathered on the patio, Adam handed
Michael a beer. "Always did like a good story. Cass tell
you I'm a writer? A first-class Irish legend might make a
great love story."

Cass shied away from Adam's suggestion. She wanted
to forget all about legends and feelings, but she couldn't
protest now. Jenn would be all over her with questions if
she did.

Reluctantly, she settled into a patio chair. Annie sat at
Michael's feet, and Todd chased the Johnsons' black Lab
around the yard.

Michael began his story, his brogue conjuring up
memories of the day Cass had heard him tell it at his
hearth in Glinbrendan. She saw Annie's eyes fill with
wonder. Had Cass been like that, too, so open and willing to believe?

Michael described the glorious horses raised by the
Daoine Sidh, and Annie's expression turned to adora-
tion. Love story, indeed. Michael would surely break
Annie's heart. Michael could break a heart, Cass realized suddenly, her discomfort intensifying.

Even Todd settled in to listen when Michael told about
the mischief. "Make yourself into a . . . a dog," he demanded.

Michael laughed. "The Good People only make
changes for the good, Todd."

"Then you could play with my dog."

"But who would play with you? I do not think it would be good to steal your friend."

Michael continued, his words echoing Cass's memories like music. How vividly she remembered the O'Sheas, their home full of noise and laughter, a home like the Johnsons'. So different from the lonely hush of the houses she'd grown up in.

When she'd gone to live with her grandparents, noise and clutter—and imagination—weren't allowed. Perhaps that was why she loved the Johnsons, their home always so full of living and loving, just as the O'Shea home had been and just as she wanted hers to be someday. The thought startled her. She'd never allowed herself to dream of a family before.

Michael finished his story. "In Glinbrendan, 'tis said a *Daoine Sidh* is visible only in the presence of believers."

"Then you must believe in Michael, Aunt Cass, because I could see him when you came in," Annie declared.

Michael watched Cass. Under his scrutiny, she held her tongue. Annie believed, and she thought Cass believed, too, that Cass was a grown-up who still believed in magic.

If only she could live up to Annie's admiration. But she couldn't. Believing had brought her nothing but heartache, and it would do the same for Annie. She had to tell Annie so, and she had to remind herself.

Annie's expectant face made Cass wince with guilt. Surely she, the daughter of Molly O'Neil, couldn't destroy Annie's belief. Surely she wasn't capable of shattering such trust. She'd never denied Santa Claus or the Easter Bunny to Annie. Then why the Good People?

Avoiding Michael's eyes, Cass said, "Yes, Annie, I believe in Michael." Let someone else crush Annie's faith.

"I knew it, I knew it." Annie jumped up and ran to him. She grasped his hands and danced in front of him, singing, "I do, too. I do, too. I believe in Michael."

"But Annie, you haven't heard the best part." Michael recaptured Cass's focus, his eyes deep blue and questioning despite his easy grin. Cass shifted uneasily.

"Tell me." Annie sat again at his feet.

His gaze lingered on Cass. "In Glinbrendan we know that when a *Daoine Sidh* is deeply and truly loved, he will be visible all the time. He will become a real person."

"Oh." Annie's face fell.

"What is it, Annie? You don't like the end of my story?"

Cass watched Michael take Annie's chin in his hand and experienced a strange agitation.

"You wouldn't be able to disappear anymore," Annie said. "You wouldn't have any fun. You'd be just like all the other grown-ups." She sounded crestfallen.

"I hope you're wrong, Annie." Michael spoke so softly, Cass could barely hear. "But you needn't fret, because it hasn't happened yet."

With a look of supreme relief, the girl jumped up and began to dance again. Cass let her breath out slowly.

"So make yourself disappear," Todd insisted.

Michael glanced down from fumbling with the beer can. "I can't disappear." Once again, merriment danced in his eyes.

"Aw, man, I knew it. You were just making it all up." Todd buried his face in the dog's neck.

Where was Michael going with his story now? Hadn't he created enough unrealistic expectations and feelings?

"How can I disappear, Todd, when all these people here believe in me?" The crevices deepened around his mouth.

"Nuts." Todd gathered his sixty pounds and six years of cynicism and rose to leave. Michael reached toward him.

"Todd, before *you* disappear, would you be so kind as to open this for me?" Michael handed him the beer can.

With a sigh of extreme imposition, Todd popped the tab, broke it free and handed them both back. Michael's fingers danced. In a flash, both the can and the tab disappeared.

"Hey! How'd you do that?" Todd demanded.

"Magic." Another spate of flying fingers and Michael produced the tab from behind Todd's ear. While the boy marveled, the beer can miraculously reappeared. "Remember, Todd. You have to believe."

Cass pushed up from her chair and sped toward the kitchen. "I'll start getting the food ready, Jenn."

All afternoon, Cass stewed over Michael's story. Now curled up in the family room with Jenn, listening to Annie and Todd help the men clean up in the kitchen, she still brooded. About the story. About Michael.

Michael persuaded his listeners to believe his story. Then, by the very terms he explained, he'd always be visible to them. How clever, this Irish riddle. No doubt Michael charmed many a maid with it. She'd almost succumbed herself once. She'd almost succumbed today.

She'd come to the Johnsons to regain perspective, but the attempt had failed dismally. She'd intended the visit to focus her away from Michael, to submit her emotions to a good dose of reality. Instead, she'd been reacting to him all afternoon like a handball ricocheting around in a court. She couldn't deny she was attracted to him. More than that, she was drawn to him.

She wanted him.

"So tell me about Blake at the airport." Jenn's request jarred Cass as if her friend had snuck up on her. "Were you surprised?"

Blake. Of course, she should be thinking about Blake. He would put her back on track.

"By the way, Cass, I heard that old B S and B is having a big party tomorrow. Are you going?"

"Darn! I forget." Cass rose from the sofa and checked her watch. "I've got to call Blake."

"Cool it. Not till you tell why." Jenn grinned.

"Blake called this morning to invite me. Practically insisted. He invited Michael, too. Can you believe that? I've got to call and tell him no."

"Why?"

"Because, my father... Michael... I have work to—"

"Cass, your father's taken care of, and you don't need to spend tomorrow brooding. It's not healthy. Besides, Blake probably invited Michael so he could check out the competition."

"Competition? Michael's not—"

"Not bad at all." Jenn's grin expanded. "You're going to that party, Cass. I won't take no for an answer." Rising, she yelled, "Adam! Bring Michael to the guest bedroom. We're going shopping."

Cass followed her friend down the hall, protesting all the way.

Jenn ignored her as she slid the closet door open. Second's later, Michael and Adam entered the room. "Michael, you're about Adam's size—three years ago." She patted Adam's belly. "Here. I always liked this outfit."

She handed Michael a lightweight ivory sports jacket and a pale aqua shirt that reminded Cass of sea waves.

Michael stood in front of the full-length mirror, holding the jacket closed at the button. He looked pleased. Cass stared at the transformation. The ivory jacket accented his dark good looks. She could imagine what the shirt and pleated trousers would add.

"It's a grand coat, Adam, but sure you'll be wanting to wear it yourself."

Adam chuckled. "I'll never get this body into that again. Besides, I wasn't invited—thank God. Just wait till you tell your story to a pack of accountants. If you get them to believe, I'll buy you suds for the rest of the year." He shook with laughter.

"How can you say that when the two best women in your life are accountants?" Cass protested.

"You're right, Cass." Adam hugged her. "But you and Jenn are different. Really different!" he added, ducking the pillows Jenn and Cass hurled from the bed.

When they were leaving the Johnsons, Annie insisted on giving Michael a goodbye kiss, but Todd barely consented to shake his hand. Michael walked beside Adam to the car, the borrowed clothes slung over his shoulder. Cass and Jenn followed.

"Cass, you're sure you don't want us to come with you to the cemetery?"

"I'm sure, Jenn. I just want to say goodbye to Dad once more. And Michael will be there."

"I like Michael, Cass."

Cass avoided Jenn's eyes. "I do, too, Jenn. He's . . . a good friend. But my future's with Blake. Right?"

Jenn hugged Cass. "Blake's not a bad catch, but I don't think you've been paying attention. Michael's one of the Good Ones. If I were you, I wouldn't let him disappear."

The buzz of cicadas droned in the muggy twilight as Cass pulled the car off the road and parked. The gate to Green Oaks Cemetery stood firmly closed, but no fence enclosed the grounds, so they walked to the plot.

The late-summer evening glowed with a golden light, lending a fairy-tale aura to the scene. Wherever Michael went, his presence seemed to cast a spell.

Not that Michael represented the unreal anymore. Even so, he was still the antithesis of everything she'd known her father to be. The fact that the two men had become friends meant her father had changed. Wil Kohlmann had reached out for a friend, had let his heart lead, just as she'd done in bringing him home to be buried. It meant he'd be glad she brought him to his beloved Molly. He would have approved. Cass had made the right decision after all.

She stood beside the mound of new earth, happy in the knowledge that her father had finally accepted her story, had accepted her. With Michael's help, she'd been able to accomplish what she'd sought—to bring her father and mother together again. And in doing so, she'd found peace within herself.

Michael stepped to her side. Remembering that grief for her father belonged not only to her, she shared his silence. Together they watched the light fade from the sky.

At last, he turned and drew her along a path beside the hedgerows. "Stay a while, Cass. 'Tis an evening you'll want to remember." He strolled quietly beside her, leaving the night full of its own sounds. Above, the sky darkened and the lights of uncountable stars pierced the blackness.

"Look, Cass," he murmured, pointing upward.

She followed the line of his arm until she saw the familiar pattern of stars. "The Big Dipper."

"And there. Your father called that 'Little Dipper.' "

She looked from the stars to Michael and found him watching her. The spell she'd perceived before rose like mist. Michael's nearness enveloped her.

"Look there, Cass." He pointed halfway up the sky. "Your father used to say, 'There's my Cassie-o.' "

"What did he mean?" Cass gazed at Michael's angular profile, edged in white light.

"See that upside-down W? Your father said that's Cassiopeia. He told me he liked to imagine that when he looked at it, you were looking at it, too."

"Cassie-o," she said the word with wonder. "He used to call me that when I was small." The memory surprised her. "Communication through the stars. I can't imagine my father ever thinking like that."

Michael regarded her a long time. Could it possibly be uncertainty she detected in him? At last, he withdrew a small tissue-wrapped package from his pocket. Taking her hand, he laid the small parcel gently in her palm.

"For Cassie-o." He hesitated, as if wanting to say more, then folded her fingers around the gift and pulled away.

An unexpected chill shuddered through her. She looked up to be sure he still stood there. Don't be silly, she chided. Yet, her fingers trembled.

She'd seen the package before, at the Shannon shop. It was for someone special, he'd said, but he offered it to her.

"Go on, open it, Cass."

"No, Michael, I can't." She didn't want him to try to make her feel better. She didn't want a gift of sympathy—especially when he'd intended it for someone else.

"Faith, Cass." He took her hand. "Open the paper. I know what you're thinking, but I bought the gift for you. You're very special, Cass. I share your father's opinion."

In his eyes she saw impatience, and amusement, and something more, feelings that tempted her beyond caution. Carefully, she unwrapped the tissue. From its folds a star winked up at her, making flecks of light dance in her hand.

"Oh, Michael."

He lifted the chain, letting the tiny bauble flicker in the air that vibrated between them. Opening the clasp, he slid his hands behind her head, his wrists faintly brushing her neck. Heat erupted where he touched her.

He withdrew his hands and looked down to where the star lay. Her hand rose to touch it, so cool against her skin. He reached out, too, then drew back.

A dark cold swept through her. She wanted him to touch her, she wanted to feel again the searing on her skin. She wanted his kiss. But she was crazy to feel this way. Even if Michael were real, their worlds were too far apart. Accountant and horse breeder—hers the logical, secure life of reason, his the intuitive, unpredictable life of dreams.

She saw questions in his eyes. When he looked to her mouth, she inhaled sharply and moistened her lips.

Abruptly, he turned away. "'Tis late, Cass. It's been a day of highs and lows. I'm sure you'll be wanting to get some sleep." Slowly, he walked away from her.

Michael, wait! she wanted to cry out, but hurt held the words back. Once more he'd pulled away. He didn't want to wait, he didn't want to kiss her. An emptiness filled her, like a black hole that lacked the power to pull him back.

Struggling for control, she watched his retreat. Of course. She knew. Their mission had ended. They'd brought her father home, and as soon as he paid his debt, Michael would leave. She'd intended that from the very beginning. Michael, not the Johnsons, had put her back in touch with reality.

Willing herself forward, Cass walked to her parents' graves. Her father lay deep within the cool earth beside her mother, his beloved wife.

And Cass was alone.

The apartment seemed like a prison. Cass paced about her bedroom, its walls closing in. She felt as if she were in solitary confinement.

Why did he haunt her so?

Michael had fulfilled his offer of help. He'd given her much more with the story of his friendship with her father and with the gift of the tiny star. He'd been supportive and encouraging and strong. She had no reason to feel so awful.

She listened for the sound of him. The floor squeaked under his tread, the closet doors rumbled, the bed whined with his weight until quiet settled in like an unwelcome guest.

Obviously, he had no trouble sleeping despite all that had happened. She imagined him lying on her floral sheets, fair skin contrasting with the dark curly hair of his chest, sinuous arms, slim waist...

"An idle mind is the devil's playground, Cathleen." Lord, her grandparents had said it often enough.

Michael had made it painfully clear at the cemetery that he was ready to be on his way. And *she* needed to get back to her own priorities.

She snatched up a tax law bulletin and dropped onto the bed. Just what she needed to get up to speed on the tax regs. She'd have them down cold by Monday.

Three minutes later, she sat staring at the wall.

Why had Michael turned away from her at the cemetery? He had his own woman back in Ireland—that had to be it. The answer hurt. But if he did have someone else, why had Michael given her the necklace? Why had he told her she was special?

Why the hell should she care?

She bounced off the bed. Grabbing her lavender silk wraparound robe, she slipped it over her thigh-length nightgown and yanked the sash tight. She needed a mug of warm milk. Switching off the bedside lamp, she crossed the room and opened the door.

From somewhere nearby, faint music floated in the air, an unfamiliar song with a melody lively and sweet. The quiet chords of a guitar drifted to her and a deep voice sang:

> "'Twas on a frosty night, at two o'clock in the morning,
> An Irish lad so tight, all wind and weather scorning,
> At Judy Callaghan's door, sitting upon the palings,
> His love tale did pour and this was part of his wailings:
> Only say you'd have Mister Brallaghan.
> Don't say nay, charming Judy Callaghan.''

Entering the living room, Cass caught sight of Michael outside on the small wooden deck. He'd obviously found her mother's old guitar in the closet. She hesitated, then slid onto the sofa.

"Oh, list to what I say, charms you've got like Venus,
Own your love you may, there's only the wall between us;
You lay fast asleep, snug in bed and snoring,
'Round the house I creep, your hard heart imploring."

Cass smiled sadly at the image of a snoring maiden oblivious to her stealthy suitor. If only she could be snoring instead of pacing with an unwelcome longing.

Listening to Michael's song eased her tension. Maybe his music would put her to sleep. She leaned back against the sofa and let the rhythm of the song lull her.

In time, she realized the words had changed, liltingly foreign and exotic, beautiful but without meaning. The last chord faded, and the music stopped, leaving silence that loomed like a barrier and filled her with regret.

"Would you like me to translate, Cass?"

She breathed in sharply. He'd known she was near, that she'd been listening.

"Come out, and I'll sing you an Irish ditty."

She slid her feet to the floor, then stopped.

" 'Tis a night not to be missed, Cass."

He was right. Ignoring reason, she moved to the sliding doors. Just one song, just one more look at her father's stars. She pulled her wrap close at the neck and stepped out into the night.

She slipped by Michael quickly, but he didn't look up. Silvery moonlight bathed his face, leaving shadows in the crevices worn by his smiles and shimmering on the planes of his cheeks and forehead—making him look like a statue of sculpted steel.

She moved silently to the deck railing and peered above the trees, searching the stars for the upside-down W. Michael's overpowering image filled her mind, and she willed herself not to look at him.

"The words meant this, Cass." He started singing again, his voice rich and mellow and true to the notes.

"I've got nine pigs and a sow, I've got a stye to sleep them,
A calf and a brindle cow, I've got a cabin to keep them;
Sunday hose and coat, and old gray mare to ride on,
Saddle and bridle to boot, which you may ride astride on."

She smiled up at the stars. The song flowed through her, the tune lulled her, cradled her in a cocoon of music as it wrapped around them.

The words reminded her of the great horse she and Michael had ridden together in Glinbrendan, though the animal had been no old gray mare. He'd sped at Michael's bidding, making her pulse race with fear and excitement, leaving her clutching his muscular middle—

"Would you like me to teach you?"

"Yes." She answered quickly, almost breathless from the memory, grateful for the interruption to the headlong rush of her emotions.

Setting the guitar aside, he stood. He walked to the railing several feet away, and her heartbeat stumbled. She thought he'd meant to teach her the words to the song, but instead he pointed upward.

"Adhar," his soft voice intoned. "Sky."

"Adhar," she repeated, focusing on the lesson, trying to mimic the turn and roll of his sounds.

"Gealach, moon," he pointed above them. Silently he moved a step nearer.

"Gealach," she answered. The moon's light cast an aura around him that reached out to draw her in.

"Rionnag, star," he said, directing her gaze to where the Cassiopeia constellation hung. *"Rionnag,"* he repeated, and reached to touch the tiny crystal star that shimmered on her chest where her robe had slipped open. His touch was as gentle as the whisper of a breeze, yet he left heat pulsing through her like the flickering flames of a fire.

As if sensing her conflict, he pointed down. *"Méarcoise."* He spoke more loudly, "toes," and smiled into her eyes. Taking her hand, he spread her fingers, pressing each in its turn. *"Méar."* He said more quietly, "fingers," and his touch made her tingle like the shimmer of crystal.

She thought for an instant to pull away, to put an end to this game, but his gaze caught hers and held. Mirrored there were her own tumultuous feelings. "Fingers," she said back to him, exhaling slowly, falling into the spell.

"Falt." He reached to touch her hair, combing wisps back, letting his fingers drift to the tiny hollow behind her ear and wander down her neck—sending tremors into her center.

"Srón." He brushed the tip of her nose with his finger, his face soft with smile.

"Nose." She whispered, *"srón,"* searching his face for the reassurance of his humor. Returning his smile, she followed his lead to keep the lesson light. "Whiskers?"

she asked, touching her fingertips to his chin, unable to pull away though smoke rose in his eyes.

"Feusag." His voice turned husky, and he clasped her hand, sliding her fingertips to his mouth, the rough stubble of his chin etching her skin with fire. Dreamlike, she leaned closer.

"Beul." He traced her fingers across the smooth texture of his mouth, then opened his lips and nibbled each one. "Mouth," he murmured, his tongue lisping her fingertips with the word. She melted, her strength giving way to pure molten softness.

"Is maith liom—" He hesitated, watching her eyes. He raised his hand to cup her face, his thumb slowly caressing the fullness of her lower lip. *"Is maith liom . . . pòg.* I want to kiss you."

The sound of his gentle words made her shudder. His thumb sent tributaries of fire from her lips to somewhere deep inside. "Yes," she said. "Yes." Whatever his words meant, with their beguiling Irish magic, *"Is maith liom pòg,"* she answered, not knowing what she had given herself to, only waiting in the white heat between breaths to learn.

Cupping her face, he leaned toward her. His lips brushed hers, stopping her as still as silence. What if she pulled away? he wondered. What if he left her hungering for his kiss? Before fear could grow, his mouth closed over hers, driving away all hesitation.

She sought his chest with her hands, and at her touch, his fingers slid from her face to capture her in his arms. She pressed to him, her heart filling with joy when he pulled her tighter against his hard body. A great hunger rose in her, and their mouths moved together, seeking, caressing, bruising with a pain that burned sweet.

Gently, he pulled away, and she uttered a faint cry, reaching toward him, holding him so he couldn't go away from her again. He shifted, then swept her up. She slid her hands around his neck, to hold him, to claim him, to never let him go. She searched his eyes and found desire as great as her own.

"Aye, *Té*," he crooned, nuzzling her ear while he carried her inside and across the carpet to her room. At her door, he stopped to look down at her.

"Michael," she whispered, "how do you say, 'Kiss me again'?"

"Cass, are you sure?" His arms tightened suddenly, keeping her from the kiss.

"Michael?" Fear sliced through her. If he turned away, if he rejected her again, she didn't think she could bear it. Whoever Michael might be, he stole her reason, leaving her only music and magic, only the taste of desire.

Reaching up, she kissed the small mole at the corner of his mouth. Memories of his arms, his wet shirt, his rain-drenched face in Glinbrendan flooded back to her, and she vowed she wouldn't let him disappear again.

"I'm not sure of anything, anymore," she said, kissing his cheek, running her tongue along his jaw to kiss his chin. He held her closer, his expression changing from surprise to desire. She pulled herself up and nibbled his ear. "But we could make believe," she whispered, breathing the words into his ear.

"Aye, Cathleen O'Neil Kohlmann. Believe." His mouth closed over hers, and she knew his desire matched her own. His lips bruising hers, he carried her into the bedroom.

Michael burned from the warm roundness of her body, the crush of her breasts against him when she slid from his cradling arms. She didn't unclasp her hands from behind his neck, but pressed to him, prolonging their kiss even while he feared she would pull away.

He'd seen the look in her eyes, the yielding, the incompleteness, the need. Her desire equaled his own—yet it was different. Different.

"Cass," he whispered, torn between hunger and anguish. Gently, he pulled from her kiss and slid his hands to her face while he gazed at her tenderly. The soft sheen of her skin shimmered in the moonlight, and her eyes misted with a deep sadness that struck an ache deep in his chest. He'd never wanted a woman so much. He'd never loved a woman more.

Beautiful, stubborn Cass, so fragile, so vulnerable this night as she realized her aloneness in the world. She needed comforting, and she sought it in his caress. But he mustn't take advantage of her loneliness, not this way.

He loved her. The wonder of it made him almost forget that she didn't love him. But she didn't—she only made believe. If ever she grew to love him truly, he would know the very minute her heart knew. The legend promised that.

A man could love her fiercely then. But for now, she needed the love of a friend.

"Michael?" Her eyes searched his with a yearning that pierced his soul.

"Ah, *Macusla,* my darling." He swept her up again and carried her to the bed.

Cass sensed the change in him. Just when they were flowing together, he'd hesitated. She'd seen him want her, she'd seen it in his eyes. Yet, he'd pulled away.

Tears welled up from the great cavern in her chest and pressed to escape. She sought Michael's eyes, imploring.

Why? Why did he turn away from her?

He lifted her again, his arms protective, his movements smooth. He carried her to the bed, and she imagined them moving in a dream, a dream that reeled into a nightmare.

At the bed, he laid her down and eased her to her stomach. He handled her gently, the passion gone from his touch. Carefully, he slid the silky wrap from her shoulders down to her waist. Every inch of her skin burned where his hands touched her, and the burning filled her with heartache. His firm grasp on her shoulders sent shivers of blue flame down her back and filled her with an anguish so painful, she wanted to crawl into herself and disappear.

She struggled to empty her mind, to withdraw into some silent place where his touch no longer wounded. Where the tears sliding down her cheeks healed instead of filling a great well of longing. She forced herself to think of nothing, nothing . . . nothing.

His strong hands kneaded her taut muscles, massaged, smoothed. While he worked, he hummed the same melody he'd sung with the guitar, keeping time with his hands.

Slowly, her tears subsided, the flames diminished, leaving only the longing that crept, downcast, into its dark place. Where it belonged. Where she must learn to subdue it.

Michael's voice crooned in the soft Gaelic sounds of his enchanted land. *"Croosheening,"* her mother had called it—whispering. He sang a lullaby. She willed her awareness away from him.

The words came to her from far away, and she realized she'd escaped into sleep and he'd left the room.

"For a wife till death I am willing to take ye,
But, och! I waste my breath, the devil himself can't
wake ye;
'Tis just beginning to rain, so I'll get under cover,
I'll come tomorrow again and be your constant
lover."

No, she'd dreamed the song. Michael would never sing
such words to her. She rolled over and, finding her pillow, hugged it close against her empty heart.

Chapter Nine

Cass slouched at the kitchen table, draining the last of her fourth mug of morning coffee. She and Michael had barely spoken since he'd wandered in from the guest room. His bare chest under his half-buttoned shirt reminded her painfully of last night—her body pressed to his, her eager kisses. His rejection.

How could she face him after the way she'd acted? After he'd made it starkly clear that he could take her— and leave her? She had to do something about the terrible emptiness where her heart was supposed to be.

He sat in the living room reading the paper, and she willed herself to look at him through the kitchen doorway. "Michael, it's going to be hot and muggy at the party, and you won't know anybody."

"Aye, Cass. Though I do know your Mr. Blake."

Blake. She didn't think he'd like her to miss the party.

"Will there be horses at this accountants' party, Cass?"

"I hardly think so. Probably golf...maybe swimming."

"I would like to try those."

Darn. If she took Michael, he'd only...confuse things. Confuse her. "I think you'd better spend the time finding another place to stay."

An uncomfortable pause stretched between them.

"To be sure, Cass." The energy faded from his voice. "Though I was looking forward to seeing your Mr. Blake."

Her Mr. Blake? Hardly that, but she'd better start working on it. Jenn said Blake saw Michael as competition. If she took him to the party, she could show Blake that Michael wasn't anyone to be concerned about. Better still, she could show Michael she had a life. She could show him last night meant nothing at all.

Cass directed the car up the lane to the two-story stone clubhouse and parked in the nearby lot. She left a wide berth between her and Michael as they walked up the circular driveway.

Blake, in white tennis shorts and shirt, stood on the broad front steps, his sun-bleached hair accenting his golden tan. Perfect as always, Cass thought. Behind him, Rachel Peterson stepped out, her skimpy white shorts and snug white tank top inviting stares, though her blond hair fluffed out like a curly halo.

"Where are that woman's clothes?" Michael whispered.

Cass smoothed her flowered sundress, annoyance magnifying her already bad humor. She and Michael were overdressed.

Michael turned and loped to the car. Jacket discarded, he strolled back, whistling a jig and rolling up his sleeves. Popping open another button on his aqua shirt, he rotated his shoulders, loosening everything to a comfortable slack. "'Tis grand to be here, Blake." He shook Blake's hand.

Blake nodded to his companion. "Rachel, Michael O'Shea, Cathleen's . . . friend, from Ireland."

Rachel flashed her green eyes at Michael, then turned to Blake. "We need you for the next game."

"We're coming." Blake took Cass's arm. "I'm glad to see you smiling again, Cathleen." He patted her hand, and she resisted the urge to compete with Rachel's flirting.

"By the way, you did bring other clothes, didn't you? You can't very well ride in those."

"Ride?" Cass's voice overrode Michael's.

"I had a couple horses brought over from my stables. I assumed, being Irish, you'd enjoy an outing, Michael."

"You ride, Michael?" Rachel's voice flowed, and Cass could practically hear eyelashes flapping.

"I've been known to mount a horse or two."

To Cass's surprise, Michael's expression suddenly lost its humor. He moved to her side. "I'll be spending my time with Cass this afternoon, thank you just the same."

"Don't be silly, Michael. You don't need to stay with us," Cass said hastily. He'd given her her first chance to show both men where her priorities lay.

Blake brightened. "Not a problem. If you ride, Cathleen, I'm sure I can borrow another horse."

"But I'm hardly dressed to—"

"My horses are here." Rachel offered, bestowing a sunshine smile on Blake.

"Sure, why don't you ride with us?"

Rachel redirected her sunny warmth to Michael.

The woman certainly wasted no time in divvying the men up: two for her, none for Cass. A woman with her own horses couldn't fail to entice Michael, Cass thought with annoyance.

"Then it's settled," Blake said. "I'm sure we can find clothes in the locker rooms. Now let's go check the games."

Cass slipped her arm back through Blake's, and he led them around the clubhouse to a patio by a large pool. Beyond, a game area stretched under giant maple trees.

"There you are, Blake. We need you for volleyball." George Singley, one of Blake's partners, beckoned them.

"Volleyball?" Michael looked intrigued. "'Twould be grand to learn this game."

"You must be Michael," George said. "Blake mentioned you. The lead team won't mind a beginner and an old codger." George winked. "Cass, the other team needs you."

At the edge of the sand-filled playing court, they kicked off their shoes and followed George.

The game resumed, and Cass observed that her team was inexperienced. She jumped forward to slam a ball back over the net, and, on the next return, she ran smack into Rachel.

On the other side of the net, Michael watched her. His chest was bare, trousers rolled to his knees. Though she tried, she couldn't seem to stop staring at him.

Darn. She'd missed a direct shot.

But, by God, she'd get the next one. With a smack, the ball launched, and she watched it curve toward the net, waited as it descended over her head, saw it coming— *Whump!* Saw blue sky and green leaves. Someone had tripped her!

Voices sounded far away. Movements shifted to slow motion. She couldn't catch her breath.

An arm slid around her shoulders. Held tightly, she dragged in great gulps of air. Blake felt her pulse, then pressed a cold cloth to her head, his face tight with worry. Her breathing eased, and she curled back into his arms.

Wait a minute. Blake knelt in front of her!

His frown deepened as she felt herself scooped up and held against a muscular body that flexed with laughter.

"Put me down, Michael!"

He set her down and helped steady her, laughing at the friendly jibes everyone hurled. Everyone but Blake.

"Blake, I..." What could she say? Someone had tripped her, someone with a smooth bronze leg and a halo of golden hair. But she'd spoil the party if she made an accusation.

"Cathleen, are you all right?" Blake looked distressed. "Come on," he said. "I'll walk with you. You'll want to... freshen up."

"A spectacular landing," Rachel said. "Michael, let's get a drink and you can tell me all about Ireland."

Cass stalled. Rachel was outdoing herself today. On the other hand, if Rachel claimed Michael, Cass could pursue Blake. Reluctantly, she walked ahead with him.

"Wait, Cass." Michael caught up. "I'm needing to cool off a bit, myself. Blake, I'll look after her."

She brushed aside an inkling of pleasure as Michael joined her. In the clubhouse, she left him outside the door to the men's room, aware that he watched her all the way up the stairs to the lounge.

Repairing her face and hair in front of the mirror, Cass found that mending her feelings didn't come as easily. She kept responding to the wrong man. Hardly the way to ignite Blake's passion.

Crossing to the sun-screened windows, she peered down on the patio. Where was Blake? Wherever he was, she could bet Rachel was with him. Rachel didn't restrict herself to a favorite. She made time with whichever man was close at hand.

Cass spotted their white-clad figures near the deep end of the pool. Rachel appeared to be talking, her hands gesturing dramatically. Suddenly, her movements faltered. She glanced from side to side. What was going on?

Rachel's gyrations enlarged. She teetered on the edge of the pool, her mouth open in a shout that Case couldn't hear. Then she tilted backward, and, arms and legs splayed, she crashed into the pool.

It almost looked as if . . . she'd been pushed!

Cass dashed to the door. No one appeared in the hall below. She hesitated outside the men's room. Was Michael still in there?

She raced down the hall. Shoving the door open, she catapulted into his arms.

"Where would you be going in such a hurry now, Cass?" He made no move to separate from her.

She practically jumped away from him. "Michael, where were you? What's going on?"

"It seems your friend Rachel fell into the pool."

"She's not my— How could she fall into the pool? How did *you* get so wet?"

How had he? She hadn't seen him near the pool, yet blotches of wetness darkened his shirt and pant leg. "Where were you when Rachel fell in?" Somehow she knew Michael had played a part in Rachel's disaster.

"I went to get a drink, Cass." He pointed to a water fountain at the edge of the patio. "I thought it was for drinking, but seems better for cooling off." The laughter in his eyes was challenging.

Cass absolutely had to ignore the part of her that wanted to climb back into his arms, that wanted to laugh out loud and cheer Rachel's unexpected dip. She'd seen Rachel fall with her own eyes, and yet... "Michael...?"

"What would you be thinking, Cass?" His grin invited her into mischief.

To her dismay, a huge part of her wanted to join him.

"Miss Kohlmann?" A young man approached and handed them each a stack of clothes. "Mr. Brockman said he'd meet you at the bridle path. I'll show you the locker rooms."

"Michael—"

"Mustn't keep your friends waiting, Cass." He directed her to follow the man. "We'll talk of such matters later."

Blake paced the bridle path next to the railing where three horses stood. His boots left heel marks in the dust.

"Blake, let's forget the ride." Cass meant to sound persuasive instead of pleading. She eyed the horses, careful to keep her distance. The large golden stallion snorted, jerked the reins and kicked at the other mounts.

"You were nice to think of Michael, but shouldn't you be back at the party?" She put her hand on his arm.

His tension barely eased. "I don't understand Rachel's fall. And now, apparently Michael doesn't want to ride."

"I think you're right. Let's take the horses back. I've never seen the stables." She reached for the mare's reins.

"Sure now, it's sorry we are to keep you waiting."

Cass and Blake spun in unison. A horse trotted up with Rachel astride and Michael seated loosely behind. He leaped backward, bouncing lightly to the ground.

Rachel looked stunning in her hunting outfit, her hair swept back and tightening into ringlets. But Michael looked absolutely roguish. He wore tight, faded jeans that defined his muscular thighs much too clearly. His half-buttoned shirt shimmered a satiny lilac color with fringes across the yoke and down the sleeves.

Cass tugged her gaze away, but not before she caught his flash of humor.

"Kow-a-bun-ga Dude? What language is this, Cass?" He read from the front of her oversize Tee-shirt, hanging down to where her knees were hidden by the baggy jeans.

She'd had to roll the legs of the borrowed jeans and gather the huge waist with a belt. The clothes and the high-top sneakers probably belonged to someone's son, someone with a friend named Rachel. Which was why Rachel looked like Queen of the Hunt while Cass came off like Harpo Marx. There was no danger of arousing Blake's passion in this getup. Maybe she should try for pity.

Michael strode to the large stallion. The animal's ears slanted back. Jerking its head, it pawed the ground.

"Better be cautious, Michael," Blake warned. "He's slow to warm to strangers. Gets downright ugly at times. I thought you could ride the pinto. Cass can ride the mare."

Michael held out his hand. The steed snuffled, then licked its large salmon-colored tongue across his palm. Michael laughed a slow rumbling approval.

Slowly, he raised his hand to stroke the animal's nose, talking quietly in words that were exotic and foreign. The horse's ears shot forward, and he nudged Michael's shoulder. Michael chuckled, patting the animal's neck.

"I believe we'll do just grand."

"Suit yourself, but don't say I didn't warn you." Blake scowled. "Go ahead. I'll help Cathleen."

"I can manage. Let's make this a short ride, okay?" She pulled up onto the saddle and watched with alarm as Michael's horse fought his weight, backing up and rearing.

He urged the animal away from the others, talking quietly with the same foreign sounds that had cast a spell over her the night before. Words that had set her up for a fall.

"You're good with horses, Michael," Rachel said. "You'll have to hunt with us sometime." She reined in next to him.

Cass sat up straight and urged her horse beside Blake's, smiling to demonstrate that he was her sole interest. She'd take no falls today.

Blake led them along the bridle path until they came to a juncture where a trail led into the woods.

"Is anyone up for something a little more exciting?" Rachel called from behind Cass.

"Aye, lead on, lass," Michael replied.

Rachel spurred her horse ahead, trotting into the trees.

Show-off, Cass thought. She nudged her horse forward, keeping pace with Blake's. Soon, the faster gait pinched a stitch in her side. She gritted her teeth.

"Ready to step it up, Michael?" Rachel shouted back.

"Sure now, I don't think Cass—"

"I'm fine. Go ahead, Michael. I'll bring up the rear."

Michael's horse reared, neighing with what sounded like sheer joy. He dashed by her, roared past Blake and stormed into the trees.

"Cathleen, I can't let Michael go off on that horse."

"Go ahead, Blake." She waved him away, trying to look carefree.

"Don't leave the path," he called back to her.

Grateful for the chance to slow, she reined the mare to a walk. No point in bruising her bottom. She had no desire to watch grown men chase a yuppy siren through the woods. The party was not turning out the way she'd hoped.

Before long, the hoofbeats faded, leaving her surrounded by the buzz of cicadas. In the shade, the heat abated. A tremor shimmered down her back. She was alone.

Nudging the little horse to a trot, she searched for hoofprints or broken branches. Uncertainty made her stop. No sounds came to her except the life of the woods. A twinge of concern needled.

She turned her horse in a circle, searching for a trail. Could she really be lost on country club grounds? Being lost could be embarrassing, but not dangerous. Eventually, she'd run into a fence or a path, either one of which would surely lead back to the clubhouse.

But she'd rather find Blake. She'd even settle for Rachel. At least the two of them knew the trails. But Michael didn't.

Michael was out there somewhere riding that ill-tempered beast. Across land he didn't know, full of branches and rocks and hidden holes. Michael could be in danger. Blake had been concerned enough to go after him. She didn't feel good about the implications of that.

Come on, Cass, she chided herself, this is a pastoral scene, not an obstacle course. Country club bridle paths could hardly be considered life-threatening.

The moment the words took shape in her mind, dread stabbed through her. Riding a bad-tempered horse in the woods *could* be. It was what had killed her father. A spooked horse, a rock hidden on the path . . . a fall . . .

Suddenly, she knew fear. She turned her ears for the sounds of horses, urged her own mount forward. "Michael?" she murmured. The woods swallowed her voice.

"Michael?" She put all her breath into the shout, yet it seemed to fade into the shadows. Where could he be? What if something had happened to him? What if—

There. Hoofbeats. "Michael?"

"Cathleen."

"Blake! I'm over here." She waved her arms.

He emerged through the trees. A deep frown knotted his face. Rachel charged through behind him.

"Where's Michael?" Cass demanded.

"Thank goodness I found you, Cathleen. I thought you both were lost."

"He should have followed me." Rachel sounded peeved.

"You mean you don't know where his is?" Cass exclaimed.

"I couldn't keep up with him," Blake answered. "He rode like a banshee. I followed his noise, but when I caught sight of the horse, he wasn't on it."

"He fell? Blake, we've got to find him."

"I've looked, Cathleen. We both did. His horse took off through the trees. We followed, but I couldn't find any sign of Michael. Strange, though. Not like a runaway..."

Cass's mind raced. "Maybe if three of us look."

"I don't want you getting lost, too." Blake sounded defeated, and he looked genuinely concerned.

"I thought he rode better than that," Rachel groused.

"Even the best rider can have trouble on a strange mount," Cass snapped. "Blake, let's go organize a search."

"Exactly. But I couldn't leave until I found you Cathleen." He gave her a halfhearted smile. "I hope nothing serious has happened to your... friend."

"So do I." Her throat tightened.

Rachel raced ahead of them through the trees. Cass kept her horse at a trot, ignoring the pain in her side. If only she rode like Rachel, she'd be in the lead to rally help. Michael could be hurt, seriously hurt, maybe even...

"I hear something," she shouted. Nearby, a horse crashed through the undergrowth. "Michael?" she called, knowing if he'd been thrown, he could be lying somewhere unconscious, or...

The thrashing drew nearer, and she prepared for a riderless horse to burst through the trees. Instead, she saw a glimpse of purple. The huge stallion pranced into view with Michael firmly astride.

"Michael!"

"Aye, Cass, you were wanting a word with me?" He reined in beside her, his smile fading as he searched her face.

"Michael, where were you? Are you all right?" Heart racing, she reached toward the line of blood along his jaw.

He touched it gingerly. "Just a scratch."

Shaken, she examined him for torn clothes and bruises. "Are you okay? Blake said you fell off your horse and—"

"Fell from my horse?" His puzzlement altered to understanding. "I didn't exactly fall. I... got down for a moment to... look at flowers. Like those that grow in Glinbrendan. The horse ran off, and I had a devil of a time catching him, and, sure now, here I am."

His grin returned, mischief all too apparent in his eyes. He was daring her to question his story! Suddenly, Cass knew that's exactly what he'd told, another story, one he'd made up just ahead of the words coming out of his mouth. He would embellish on it, she was sure, if she challenged him.

But he was alive. He was whole. That's what mattered. She restrained herself from hugging him.

"I knew they shouldn't worry about you," Rachel bubbled.

Blake mopped his forehead. "Sorry the horse gave you trouble, Michael. We'd better get back. It's almost time for cocktails." His words were clipped.

Cass followed Blake, turning to be sure Michael came along. Slowly, her relief gave way to vexation. Michael had given them a real scare. He'd frightened her terribly. Her hands were still shaking.

Michael caught up with them, whistling. Rachel homed in on his other side. Grudgingly, Cass watched them. They were both expert riders. Michael had the stallion well under control. He'd probably never fallen off a horse in his life.

And what about his story? She couldn't believe he'd leave a touchy horse untethered after he'd dismounted. Dismounted to look for flowers? Chased a horse around in the woods? Unbelievable.

Suddenly, she gasped. The images came to her like pieces of a puzzle. All the uncertainties she'd fought ever since she'd found Michael again: his disappearances, the elusive passport, Rachel's dive into the pool, the riderless horse. Above all, Michael's eyes—always asking her to stay near.

Was Michael one of the *Daoine Sidh* after all? If it were true, why was he playing games . . . with her life? If it were true, would he destroy everything she'd worked for?

They came to the end of the bridle path. "Will I see you at the party, Michael?" Rachel asked.

"That depends on Cass." Once more he turned that questioning gaze on her.

A gaze she would no longer let go unanswered.

"Michael, why don't you go with Blake to put up the horses?" She smiled. And waited.

"I'll be needing the time to dress for the party—"

"Then I'll go help with the horses." She struggled to keep her thoughts masked.

Michael looked to Blake, to Rachel, then back to her. "In Glinbrendan each person cares for his own mount, Cass, so I'll be coming along." His concern dissolved into the familiar lopsided grin.

Blake dismounted. "Why don't you two go dress? Rachel can help me."

"Sure, that's grand, Blake." Michael leaped down and handed over his reins. "We don't want to be late, Cass." He helped her down and tugged her away.

Outside the woman's locker room, she stopped. "I'll meet you in the foyer, unless you're coming in *here* with me, too."

He had invited her into mischief more than once this afternoon, and she was about to take him up on the challenge. They would stay for the accountants' party. She would establish a future with Blake. And before this day ended, she would learn the truth about Michael.

Chapter Ten

Cass hurried to the country club foyer, watching for Michael all the way. She had to get there before him. She intended to find out exactly when and where he could be seen. If, away from her, he disappeared. She wasn't sure just how she'd manage that, but she would. Somehow.

Stopping halfway down the hall, she peered into the foyer. No sign of him yet. This would be a good place to watch from, far enough away not to be seen, but near enough so she could detect exactly when he entered—or when he materialized. She leaned against the wall and waited.

The front doors opened. Blake's partner, Ron Barnsworth, stepped in with his wife, and immediately headed toward her. "Cass, is that you?"

So much for trying to hide. She mustered a smile.

"Waiting for Blake? Come on with us. He'll find you."

What about Michael? If she didn't stay, would he appear? Reluctantly, she joined the Barnsworths.

"Sure, if you don't mind, I'll follow right behind."

She whirled at the sound of Michael's voice. The sight of him made her almost forget her plan. The faint scratch on his jaw revived tremors of her earlier fears. Or were the tremors because he looked so good? He was dressed impeccably for the party, especially with his jacket slung over his shoulder. He must have gone to the car to retrieve it—and spoiled her chance of learning the truth about him.

"There you are!" Rachel hurried toward them as they approached the banquet room. She'd changed into a bright green sundress, her golden hair newly styled.

"Cathleen. I've been watching for you," Blake greeted her when they entered. "You look lovely." Acting very much in command again, he smiled warmly and reached for her hand.

Things were taking a decided turn for the better.

"You look good, too, Michael." Rachel brushed up against his arm. "Let's get something to drink."

Edging away from Rachel, he looked back at Cass with the familiar watchfulness she'd come to expect. Was he concerned about being away from her?

"I'll get drinks for us, too, Cathleen," Blake said. "I won't be long." He squeezed her hand.

With the three of them gone, Cass excused herself and wended her way through the crowd. Across the room, she caught sight of Rachel with Michael in tow. He scanned the room over his shoulder. *Yes, Michael, I'm still here.*

Pressing on, she maneuvered herself to the far end of the room where she could survey everything. Briefly, she checked her appearance in the wall mirrors, reached for a wisp of hair—and stopped with her hand in midair.

Mirrors. Mirrors might offer possibilities. And what about this small door next to the mirror? She turned the knob until she heard a muted click. The door slipped open a fraction. Quickly, she looked over her shoulder and searched the crowd for Michael. He stood with Rachel and the Barnsworths, his attention on the conversation.

Good! With a tug, she opened the door and stepped through, pulling it closed behind her.

She squinted in the subdued light of the narrow room. A man sat at a long console, his hands moving among the rows of switches that covered its surface.

"Yo." The man saluted her with two fingers, then turned back to the equipment in front of the windows.

Windows? She'd seen no windows outside, only... mirrors! A sound room hidden by mirrors. She could see out, but...

What a find! She stepped up the single stair and leaned over the console to look out.

"Get too close and they'll see you on the other side."

"Thanks." She hoped he couldn't see her blush. She searched for Rachel's bright green dress.

Rachel still stood with the Barnsworths. Other people had joined them, but Blake hadn't returned. She couldn't see Michael either, yet no one seemed bothered by his absence. Only Rachel kept looking from side to side. Apparently, he hadn't just evaporated, but where was he?

"Anyone in particular you want to watch?"

Reluctantly, she turned her attention to the disc jockey. He appeared younger than she'd first thought, his blond hair spiked and standing straight up on both sides of the earphone headband. He looked as if he were in a perpetual state of fright, but at least his hair wasn't pink.

"It's just fun to look," she said lightly.

"Sure." He slid one earphone up, his mouth twisting into a smirk. "You're welcome to spy as long as you want. I like a little company, especially from a foxy red-head."

She started to protest, but took a deep breath. She might as well be peeping through curtains. He'd accused her accurately, but she wouldn't act embarrassed. And she couldn't pass up such an opportunity.

Staying near the door, she looked out the windows again. A small parade moved through the crowd, Blake in the lead, followed by a bartender carrying a tray of glasses. They joined the Barnsworths' group.

Still no sign of Michael. But... if Michael *were* invisible, he could be dancing a jig in the middle of the group and no one would be the wiser. Would he suddenly reappear if she went back into the banquet room?

That's exactly what she ought to do. She pulled the door open and shot through.

The atmosphere around the Barnsworths' group didn't so much as ripple. Blake continued to distribute drinks. People continued to talk. Only when she scanned the rest of the room did she discover Michael walking toward the central entrance. Had he materialized right there when she'd entered? She hadn't moved fast enough to see.

Making her way across the room, she caught up with him just as he sauntered into the hall. He stopped in front of a painting of flying ducks and studied it intently. "One minute you're leaving me behind, and the next you're following me," he said, as if scolding the ducks. But the meaning carried straight to her. "Sure, Cass, it's more than a bit confusing."

"Where are you going, Michael? Why don't you come back to the party?" She wouldn't let him put her on the defensive.

"I will, Cass, now that you're here. Rachel's a nice lass, but after you disappeared—"

"After *I* disappeared? You're the one who—"

Hold it. She'd best not pursue that course with him. If he figured out what she'd tried to do, he might become more elusive than ever. She'd never confirm her suspicions.

"Never mind. Let's go back for dinner."

They returned to the banquet room to find bright lights flooding the dance-floor stage where George Singley stood with a microphone. Behind him, a young man in a tuxedo moved about, setting up small tables. A human-sized box, sprouting with wires and lights, dominated the right side of the stage.

"For your pleasure before dinner," George intoned, "we have The Jack of Clubs, Jack Wilson, and his magic act."

Applause rippled through the room while people hurried to claim seats at the café-style tables on the dance floor.

"Incidentally, folks," George continued, "Jack is Blake's nephew. Blake suggested we give him his big break tonight."

The spotlight found Blake, and the applause increased.

Rachel beckoned Michael to the seat beside her near the stage. Cass followed, and Blake joined them, pulling his chair close to hers.

The background music changed to rock rhythms, and the young magician swayed to the beat while he began his tricks. From a jacket pocket, he pulled a streamer of scarves followed by an enormous bouquet of flowers. Warming up, he emptied other pockets, producing a dozen eggs, one by one, and laying them carefully on a table.

He began a running patter that engaged the audience and soon had everyone laughing. From his pant legs, he produced an umbrella, a cowboy hat and two baby chicks. From the boxes on the various tables, he brought forth all kinds of colorful items, followed by a live rabbit that emerged, incredibly, from his breast pocket. He accumulated a wonderful pile almost three feet high in the middle of the stage. The music changed, and he reversed the procedure, making the same objects disappear one by one.

After a bow, the magician stepped forward. "I need a volunteer." He coaxed the girls at a front table, then moved nearer. Blake leaned to whisper in Cass's ear.

"I don't know, Blake..."

Blake patted her on the shoulder, then flagged his nephew's attention. He pointed discreetly at Michael.

Two more jokes, and the magician zeroed in. Despite Michael's protests, the young man cajoled him to the stage. "I promise you, ladies, if I make him disappear, I'll bring him right back. I know I'll be in big trouble if I don't." The women in the audience applauded.

Michael moved into the light, his smile tentative but good-natured. He shielded his eyes to search the tables below.

Feeling his uncertainty, Cass willed her assurance across the space between them. *I'm right here, Michael.* Suddenly, her heartbeat accelerated. Without realizing, Blake had created the perfect opportunity. "I'm right here, Michael," she whispered, *"but I won't be for long."*

The magician spun his spells, asking Michael questions, guiding him slowly toward the techno-crate. Checking that Blake watched the stage, Cass slipped from her seat and stole through the crowd. She reached the wall of mirrors just as The Jack of Clubs opened the box.

"Michael, if you'll step into the magic travel machine, we'll send you wherever you want to go. Las Vegas? Hawaii? Perhaps somewhere a bit more exotic, like a harem?"

"Sure, I've always wanted to see Churchill Downs."

Cass watched him shade his eyes again. His smile stalled when he looked down at the table where she'd been sitting. She saw his expression change—a flash of understanding, then a satisfied grin.

"I'm ready to go, Mr. Jack." Without a backward glance, he stepped into the box.

The young man closed the door. "Dydee, hidee, so long, be gone," he chanted.

She'd better be gone, too. Quickly, she entered the sound room, closed the door and moved up to the windows.

On stage, the magician completed his hocus-pocus and prepared to reopen the box. He waved an oversize key, mimed the unlocking of the door, and, with a sweeping flourish, swung it open.

The box appeared to be empty.

Through the window, she could see hands clapping, but silence deadened the air in the small room.

"Could you flip a switch so we can hear the magician?"

"You want to hear all that bull?" The disc jockey adjusted a switch on the console, and the sounds of the banquet room came on around them. "Good idea, at that," he said, removing the headphones and rubbing his ears. He tested for a dent in his upright hair. "Got bored out there? Glad you knew where to come for a little action."

Cass's attention fastened on the magician who pulled balloons from the empty box where Michael had stood just moments before. Some of the balloons floated with helium, some bulged with water and some exploded in white puffs of flour when they broke.

"Hold on there, Foxy. A little grand finale music, then me and you can get to know each other." The disc jockey switched on a drumroll.

The Jack of Clubs closed the box door and started his spiel to bring Michael back. Flourishing the key, he called, "Come back to us, Michael O'Shea." He swung the door open and dipped into a deep bow.

"Okay, foxy lady, come over here and tell me your name."

Cass barely heard the man's words. She could see the box clearly. It stood empty, just as she'd expected.

The magician straightened and laughed. "Ladies and gentlemen, it appears that Michael chose the harem after all. I'll need your help to convince him he does want to come back. If we could have that drumroll again, please." The young man closed the box.

"He wants the drumroll again," Cass prompted.

"Yo. More drumroll." The disc jockey reached for a switch. "This guy better hurry. My time's about up, and I got better things to do, now that you're here."

The snare drums resumed. "Ladies and gentlemen, the return of Michael O'Shea." With a sweeping gesture, the magician swung the door open.

The box stood empty.

"Ha!" Cass exclaimed, and a collective "Oooooh," rose from the audience. The first time could have been part of the act. This time, the strain on the young man's face told her what she'd suspected. Michael's disappearance wasn't an illusion.

The magician's laugh erupted almost on time. "That must be some harem. Next time, I'll go myself." The audience hooted and clapped.

"What the hell's going on out there?" the disc jockey grumbled.

"I think you'd better play the drumroll again," Cass answered, inching her way toward the door.

"Ladies and gentlemen, it's going to take some pretty potent magic to get this Irishman back. Let's have a hand for the three partners, Barnsworth, Singley and Brockman. Come on up here, gentlemen."

Oh, dear. She'd let things go too far. She'd meant to test Michael, to find out if he really came from the legend, if its lore applied to him. She hadn't meant to embarrass the magician. She hadn't intended to involve Blake.

The time had come to bring the test to an end.

Renewed laughter made her look again. The three partners and the magician stood spotlighted in utter amazement while scarves and flowers flew through the air. An umbrella popped open and bobbed into place over George Singley's head just in time to protect him from a floating water balloon that appeared to self-destruct in midair, cascading water like fireworks.

"What the . . . ?" The disc jockey stood.

Cass winced when she saw the eggs ascend from a table. Michael wouldn't . . . ? Yes, he would. The eggs met in midair and cracked into slimy ooze that barely missed Blake's head but slid down his shoulder when he ducked in the wrong direction. Balloons followed, some exploding into white clouds of flour, others splattering water from where they detonated on the floor. A tiny yellow chick emerged from Blake's pant leg, and multicolored balls bobbed through the air as if held aloft by an invisible juggler.

"Hey, Foxy, looks like the magician's gonna keep that audience busy for a while. Com'ere and let's me and you make friends." The disc jockey sidled toward her. Alarmed, she sidestepped, groping for the door. He grabbed her wrist and pulled her forward. "Let's have a little kiss."

"No. Wait." She pushed against him and teetered backward, losing her balance on the edge of the step. Quickly, she braced herself on the console, bumping several switches, struggling to regain her footing.

"I have to leave." She tugged, trying to pull free from his grasp. "Let me go."

"You don't have to go yet. We haven't gotten acquainted. Com'ere." He yanked her against him.

"Let—me—go! Michael, where are you when I really need you?"

She strained away from the man's looming face to search desperately out the window. The scene there stopped her cold. Everyone in the ballroom stared toward the mirrors.

With a crash, the door flew open. "Is this a private fight, or can anyone join in?" Michael bounded up the step and across the floor to smash the disc jockey in the jaw. The man sagged silently to the floor.

"Sure, it's a good thing you called me, Cass, or I wouldn't have known you needed me. Are you all right?" He reached for her.

Without hesitation, she slid into his arms. "Michael, how did you—? You could hear?" She looked into his face, so near, so handsome, his cerulean eyes full of feelings she dared not let herself consider.

"Michael, up there on the stage ... I mean, I can't believe you had the nerve to—"

Laughter filled the room like a sound track. Through the window, she saw faces crinkled in hilarity, including three of the four men on stage, all of whom dripped with water and egg and flour.

"I don't even believe this, Michael."

"Are you sure now, Cass?" he challenged.

Held there in the warmth of his embrace, sharing laughter, sharing heartbeats, she could no longer deny him. She did believe.

"Come, Cass. I think we'd best set things right."

Michael helped the disc jockey up. "Sure, now, you'll be needing a chair until your head clears. It's sorry I am that I hit you so hard, lad, but the lass didn't take a liking to you. Better I that hit you than she. She can knock a man into the next county if she's a mind to."

Laughter rumbled through the speakers.

Cass tugged Michael to the door, and they pushed through the crowd that had gathered outside. To her dismay, instead of going to the exit, Michael led her onto the stage.

She flinched at the sight of the bedraggled men sponging their clothes with wet napkins. George and Ron laughed uproariously, but Blake refused to look at her.

Michael spoke into the microphone, and the audience quieted. The spotlight sought him, then expanded to include the soggy men and Cass.

"Ladies and gentlemen," said Michael, mimicking the magician's inflection, "'twas a grand time at the harem, but it appears I missed a bit of malarkey while I was gone." He circled the dripping men studiously and the laughter rose.

"I think you've seen a magic show that would put leprechauns to shame—and lads who are the best of good sports." Michael began to clap, and very soon everyone in the room joined in, shouting approval. George and Ron stepped forward smiling. Reaching back, they dragged Jack and Blake up for a bow. Blake smiled woodenly.

"I've enjoyed my time here at this American country club. I thank you all, and I thank Mr. Blake, and I especially thank this lovely lass."

In one deft movement, he pulled her into his arms and kissed her. Not a simple appreciative peck, but a real kiss. He held her tight and claimed her lips, challenging her, daring her to pull away.

And though every rule of her Kohlmann upbringing shouted protest, demanded that she stop, somehow she simply didn't listen. At the touch of his lips, desire reawakened, curled through her, made her yield. Her hands slid around his neck and wove into his hair, her lips gave answer as she sought the shape of his kiss.

Breathless, they pulled apart, laughing at the cheering crowd. Michael led her from the spotlight and through the applause, down the hall and outside into the twilight.

With Michael at her side, she flew. Warm honey bubbled inside her. The night settled in, and each star awakened to wink down exclusively on her.

They reached the car, and he stopped, touching her cheek with his palm, sending starlight shimmering through her. He scanned her face with a look that held more than she knew how to read. "You're not like all the other grown-ups, Cass. You still believe in magic."

She believed. She couldn't deny it any longer.

And that magic had just ruined her life.

Chapter Eleven

"Michael, life isn't a game. Magic isn't real."

So Cass had finally decided to talk to him after her terrible silence the whole ride back to the apartment. Michael looked up to the distant moon for encouragement.

"Cass, I do not understand why you wouldn't talk to Blake when he came after you. We shouldn't have just raced away. I swear by St. Paddy, I'll hold you here in the car until you talk to me." He'd much rather hold her in his arms, but he knew such a move would send her running.

"It's easy for you to say 'believe in magic,' Michael. I'll bet you have lots of fun with it, just like tonight."

"It wasn't I who gave the poor magician lad the living bejabbers, Cass. I didn't *choose* to disappear, you know."

"I know." She sounded miserable. "And Blake probably thinks I was involved in your...performance."

"Then why did you not stop to explain when he came after you?" He leaned toward her, longing to touch her unhappy face.

"Explain what, Michael? That you're a character from an Irish legend? He wouldn't believe me, and trying to explain wouldn't help. You've already destroyed my future."

"Destroyed your future, Cass? Is Blake what you'd planned for your future?" He dreaded her answer.

"I . . . planned a lot of things. Like a reputation for sound reasoning, and predictability, and not believing in—"

"Sure now, Blake understands a wee bit of mischief."

"A wee bit of mischief? You call kissing me in front of the whole company a 'wee bit of mischief'? And the eggs? And the water balloons and—?" She stopped, her eyes anguished. "Do you understand that your . . . magic will probably cost me my job? It's one thing to have fun, Michael, but these are serious people. You seriously compromised my boss."

"Ah, Cass." Frustration made him sigh. He could break the bad habits of a filly more easily than he could overcome Cass's bad training. He'd thought she'd finally broken free of the Kohlmann upbringing. She'd returned his kiss with more than a little passion. She'd been a woman who wanted magic. But now she'd put the harness on again, for love of another man.

No, not even love. He could see she didn't love Blake.

"I'm afraid your father had reason to be concerned."

"My father?" Her breath caught in her throat. "Michael, you lied to me. My father couldn't have known you."

"But he did, Cass." He would tell her now. If she couldn't love him, if she couldn't accept the belief still alive inside her, at least he could give her some peace.

"After your father sent you back to St. Louis, he closed himself off from everyone. Only the last few years did he begin to seek out your aunt and uncle as friends.

"With them, your father came to understand the woman he'd married. 'Mad Molly O'Neil,' he used to say, but I knew he said it with love.

"He understood you better, too, Cass. He loved you. He missed you greatly. He didn't want to be separated from you. He wanted to break down the wall he'd built by not believing in you. He wanted to believe . . . as you did.

"After your uncle told him the story of the *Daoine Sidh,* I think each time he came to the stud farm, he searched for me. That day in the stable when I spoke to him, he finally let loose of his logic. He let his heart see. That's when we become friends."

"My father *knew* you were . . . ? He believed? Why didn't he tell me? Why didn't he let me know that I . . . ?"

Her anguished questions hung in the air, making him ache for her. If only he could comfort her. "Your father was afraid, Cass, afraid you'd turn away. He accepted the openhearted lass you'd been, but he feared your grandparents had finished too well the job he'd started with you. I told him believing couldn't be disciplined away." He paused, discovering a new uncertainty in himself.

"I don't know anymore." He watched the conflict in her eyes. "You're like a butterfly, Cass, with a rock tied to its leg." The silence stretched into dark discomfort.

"Those are pretty words, Michael." Her voice sounded husky, almost sad, as if she longed to cast away the burden.

He watched her draw in a slow breath, pull herself up straight. "You may be able to get away with words like that where you come from. But you can't go around talking blarney and acting like a leprechaun in civilized society." She reached for the door handle.

"*Rionnag.*" He spoke the word softly, imploringly.

"What?"

"*Rionnag.* Don't you remember, Cass? It means star."

Abruptly, she snapped the car door open. "No, Michael. I don't remember any of the words you taught me." She slammed the door behind her.

Frustration expanded in his chest. He shouldn't have reminded her of the closeness they'd shared. Last night, she'd wanted to break loose, to give herself to their kisses. He'd only meant to touch that part of her again.

"Cass, wait!" He dashed after her up the stairs.

Inside, glaring lights filled the empty kitchen and a lonely ringing filled the air.

"Cass, will you answer the telephone?" The sound persisted. Hesitantly, he picked up the receiver. "Hello?"

"Hello? Cathleen? I need to talk to you. Cathleen?"

"Blake, this is Michael. Can you—" Click.

Where was that woman? How could she be so unwilling to hear her heart? He stomped through the apartment and pounded on her bedroom door. "Cass, if it's Blake you're wanting in your future, you'd best be answering the telephone for 'twas he that called, and he cannot hear me."

Her door jerked open. "I don't want to talk to Blake and I don't want to talk to you."

"Cathleen O'Neil Kohlmann, you're more obstinate than a mule, and a mule more than the devil," he declared, his anguish mounting.

"Michael, just leave me alone."

"Leave you alone? Sure now, if that's what you're wanting, I'd best be leaving."

"Yes, go. Leave! Get out of my life."

He braced himself for the door to slam, but a sudden spark flared in her already fiery eyes.

"Disappear!" she shouted. Then the door crashed shut.

If he were a cursing man, he'd burn St. Paddy's ears. He stalked away, clenching his fists. Pegeen had told him, "What cannot be had is just what suits." Sure, that's all that accounted for his fury at this lovely, misguided woman who'd forgotten how to fly. He couldn't allow himself to love her anymore.

Another of Pegeen's sayings came to him. "To die and to lose one's life are much the same."

Much the same as loving. If loving held this much pain, he didn't want to be real.

Cass stood behind the shuddering door and fought her trembling. She didn't want to see Michael. She couldn't bear to see his stormy eyes, to hear his soft brogue. The story he'd told her about her father should have freed her, should have brought her closer to Michael, but she couldn't stop remembering how he'd turned her life upside down. Again.

Michael said she had a rock tied to her leg, but he was wrong. She'd sought a rock to *stand* on, the solid ground of reason. This time Blake would be the one to question her stability, the one who would send her away.

In the darkness, she curled onto the bed, burying her head in a pillow to muffle Michael's sounds. Most of all, she didn't want him to remind her of last night's lesson, of the seductive Irish words that had led to kisses, kisses he'd turned away from.

God, she didn't want to feel like this. So much confusion, so much pain. She'd lost all sense of logic. She'd lost control of her life.

Suddenly, she stiffened. The doorbell? Had Michael locked himself out? If so, he could just stay out. No one could see him anyhow. Miserable, she closed her eyes.

The bell sounded again, becoming a persistent *ding-dong* that matched the throbbing in her head. She jumped up, stormed through the apartment and jerked the door open.

"Michael, will you sto—Blake!"

"Cathleen, I have to talk to you. Please let me come in." He pressed into the room.

Cass turned away. "Blake, I'm so sorry for the embarrassment we caused you. I'll clean my desk out first thing in the morning."

"Cathleen?" He touched her shoulder.

Slowly, she turned and focused on a shirt button.

"I tried to catch you in the parking lot. I didn't want you to think I was angry. I don't know how he did it, but Michael's part of the magic act stole the show. Everyone raved, 'What's happened to stuffy old B S and B?' George told me if I don't give you a promotion and put Michael in charge of parties, he'll have *my* job."

Cass stared up at his bleak face in astonishment.

"There's more." He hesitated. "I...apologize for the way I acted. I'm not a good loser, Cathleen, but I assure you, I won't let that interfere with your job."

"Loser?"

"If you love him, then I'm sure Michael's a fine man."

"Blake, I don't... He's... Blake, what are you saying?"

"Cathleen, I'd hoped that you and I . . . that we might build a future together. I didn't know you already had Michael."

"I don't already—"

"But I thought . . . It looked like—"

"Well, it isn't."

Blake's face altered to a hopeful smile. "Don't say another word. Take the day off tomorrow, get rested up, get your father's affairs in order. Then maybe we can give it another try." He bent and kissed her lightly on the cheek. "You've made me very happy, Cathleen. May I pick you up for dinner tomorrow night?"

"I guess . . ."

"About seven." He squeezed her hand, then left, closing the door behind him.

Blake hadn't questioned her sanity at all. He still wanted to see her.

And Michael had overhead the whole conversation. Which provided the perfect opportunity to tell him he had to leave tomorrow.

She walked to the guest room. The bed lay empty, the spread unrumpled. Where was he? A finger of concern touched her. Had she stopped believing? Had he become invisible? Uncertainty wrapped around her.

She rushed to the kitchen, and her heart faltered. Michael's finely carved wooden box lay open on the table, coins and bills scattered across the top.

At the back door she called, "Michael, are you out there?" Only the crickets answered.

Hesitantly, she retraced her steps to the table where she picked up the box and stroked the smooth shamrock pattern. She stared at the coins and saw that they formed a pattern, almost like . . . a word.

"Gaol," she whispered. Not a familiar sound, not one she'd ever heard Michael say. But the short syllable echoed in the hollow of her chest. She knew what the word meant.

It meant Michael had gone.

Cass squinted one eye at the clock on the nightstand. Ten till six. She'd been awake all night, and her thoughts still roiled like the black clouds brewing outside.

Monday morning. Time to get ready for work. That's what she'd come to at three-thirty a.m.—that legends and logic didn't mix. That she should get on with her life. Everything she'd worked for waited at Barnsworth, Singley and Brockman.

A flash of lightning penetrated the gloom.

Michael's gone.

She sat up. Wrapping her robe around her, she rushed to the kitchen. Thunder echoed in the distance.

Michael's word still spoke to her from the table—*gaol,* his farewell. She turned and hurried away.

In the bathroom she adjusted the shower and stepped in. The storm outside rumbled and churned, matching the agitation of her thoughts.

The pieces of her life had finally fallen into place. Out of the chaos of the last days had come assurance of everything she'd struggled to maintain, her sanity, her job, Blake. Most important, proof that her father had believed in her.

This should be a momentous day.

A white slash of light stabbed through the window.

Michael's gone.

Michael. An imaginary character from an old Irish story, who'd stepped out of a fairy ring to fill her life with magic. How could she possibly deal with that logically?

·And her father, a man whose reality had been cast in concrete. He'd *chosen* to see Michael, to believe in him. How could she ever integrate the image of who her father used to be with the man he had become?

And Blake, the serious-minded numbers man who apologized because he couldn't find humor in a "wee bit of mischief." Why did that bother her so?

She knew. In the dark of night, she'd finally accepted that Michael had answered her test of the legend with his own legendary mischief. Like the comedian who smashed watermelons, he'd created mayhem—with malice toward no one. Then he'd made amends for his fun, gone back on stage to praise everyone, especially Blake. He'd even apologized to the disc jockey.

And then he'd kissed her. A kiss so sweet, so wondrous, she could never forget. Yet, how could she live with only the memory of desire?

Desire? Yes. She'd wanted Michael. But not as part of her life. She'd *told* him to leave.

Abruptly, she turned off the shower faucets.

She'd denied her feelings. Without realizing it, she'd become like her father, the way he used to be. Inaccessible...rejecting...for the sake of logic and reason. All of the qualities she'd hated in him, she'd made her own.

She stepped from the tub and groped in the steam for the towel. Briskly, she rubbed herself dry and dressed, then hurried to the living room. Locating a small volume on the bookshelf, she carried it to the kitchen where Michael's message called to her from the table.

She flipped the English-Irish Gaelic dictionary open to the B's and ran her finger down the page. "Belfry...belie..." There. "Believe—believing—*ag creidsinn*..*

Ag creidsinn? She stared at the words. Not *gaol?*

Sadness engulfed her. She'd been so sure Michael wanted to tell her to believe. To keep on believing.

Slowly, she closed the book. A small act, but full of meaning. A part of her life had come to an end. She needed to start a new story.

She carried the book to the living room and knelt to put it back on the shelf. Her knee rested near a smattering of small dark spots on the carpet. She reached to touch one.

Fuzz. Irish sock fuzz. Darn. She slid onto the sofa holding the small piece of lint as if it were a tiny mouse. Tears filled her eyes, and she heard the rain splatter against the window, a wind-driven rain like the storm in Glinbrenden the day she first saw Michael. Her heart winced.

Michael had gone, just as she'd told him to, leaving a message she couldn't fathom and money she didn't want. He'd gone into the world both invisible *and* broke. Could he survive under those conditions? Especially in such a storm? Without Glinbrendan nearby to offer shelter?

What if, outside of Ireland, without her, he disappeared . . . forever?

No! She couldn't bear to lose another loved one. She couldn't—

Loved one. She loved Michael.

The moment she thought it, she knew. She loved Michael Padraig Brendan O'Shea. She, Cass Kohlmann, daughter of Mad Molly O'Neil, *loved* one of the Good People of Irish legend.

Crazy Cass Kohlmann . . . whose new story opened with her return to a prestigious accounting firm. The middle part included a partnership in the firm with the respect and status such a position brought. The high point would be her relationship and probable marriage to the handsome, wealthy, very down-to-earth Blake Brockman. A match that would produce attractive, well-behaved children who wouldn't be loud and wouldn't commit "wee bits of mischief" and who definitely wouldn't believe in leprechauns. And in the end, they'd all live happily ever after... Or would they?

Carefully, Cass slid the sock fuzz into her pocket. She rose and walked slowly to the kitchen. Picking up the phone, she punched in the familiar numbers.

"Mary? Cass Kohlmann. Would you give Mr. Brockman a message? Tell him I have to break our date for tonight. Also that I'm quitting. Effective immediately. Tell him not to take it personally. I just have to go to Ireland."

Cass shifted in the plane seat, trying to get comfortable. Four hours in the air and she still couldn't sleep. She couldn't stop going over her plans.

First she'd rent a car at Dublin airport and drive to the fairy *rath*. If Michael didn't appear there, she'd try to find Glinbrendan.

She'd have to travel purely on intuition because her memories of their walk ten years ago were so uncertain. Through the pastures, down a slope, into a basin, where, nestled in its hollow, she'd find the glowing thatched-roof cottage. Glinbrendan.

Maybe Glinbrendan... if there were any truth at all about the strength of love.

She'd have to find Pegeen, her only hope of finding Michael.

But what if Pegeen told her Michael had come back to Glinbrendan to stay? He'd turned away from Cass more than once. The fact that she loved him might mean nothing to him at all.

She stared down at the dark waters below, and a cold ness swept through her. Whatever the consequences fo her, she had to learn Michael's fate.

If Pegeen told her he'd returned to Glinbrendan saf and whole, she'd offer up a joyous prayer of thanks. I Pegeen said he didn't care to see her, she'd gather th pieces of her heart and go away—somewhere.

But, please, don't let Pegeen tell her that Michael wa lost. That he was gone—forever.

Chapter Twelve

Gray clouds, thick as wool, lay cold and somnolent above the trees as if refusing even a shaft of sun for a woman so slow to understand her heart.

Cass stood inside the looming hedge of the fairy *rath*, longing to plead with the magical powers that dwelt there. One chance she'd ask, just one, to bring Michael back from wherever he might be. She'd tell him she believed. She'd tell him she loved him, even if it meant watching him turn away to disappear into the mists of Glinbrendan forever.

At least then she'd be sure he was with the *Daoine Sidh* instead of lost in some netherworld because of her. Because she'd been unwilling to accept her belief in him.

Cass strode to the center of the *rath*. "My name is Cathleen O'Neil Kohlmann. I've come to seek Michael Padraig Brendan O'Shea." She held her breath, listening beyond the rustling leaves for some whisper that told of his presence.

Painful silence answered, mocking her plea with an emptiness the chill wind couldn't dispel. Shivers coursed down her back, as if a lost soul had brushed against her.

She paced the perimeter of the ring, searching every shadow, every hollow. "If you're here, Michael, show me you're all right. I promise, if you ask me to, I'll leave." Somewhere above, a dove cooed its sad hollow notes, their meaning unbearable. Michael wasn't there.

At the narrow opening in the hedge, she looked back once more, then climbed through, oblivious of the thorns that snagged her jeans and tore at her denim blazer.

No sun broke through the heavy indifferent clouds. She searched for familiar landmarks to guide her in the direction she and Michael had taken the day of the storm. Unsure, she pushed forward, trusting her intuition far less than she'd trusted the blue-eyed stranger who'd protected her so tenderly from the wind-driven rain that day.

She'd come close to loving him then, but she'd been sent away too soon. Away from fantasy, away from dreams, away from the magic only her heart could see. Her father's death had brought them back together. Without the journey they'd shared with her father, she might never have seen stars again. The understanding made her pain all the more sharp.

Ahead, a covey of birds fluttered into the air, stirring a flicker of hope. Maybe the birds were a sign, like the birds they'd scared up that day. "Seven for a secret," he'd said, but all too quickly the rhyme played out in her memory. "A secret never to be told."

No. She knew the secret, Michael's secret. She had to keep believing.

She began to run. The scenery hardly changed except for an occasional group of trees or a dry ravine, but suddenly her pulse skipped, and she slowed in uncertainty.

The ground had begun to slope downward—she could feel it beneath her feet, dropping away into a hollow that brought back memories of a ghostly white cottage luminous in the rain, torrents of water slucing from its steep roof.

Increasing her pace, she peered through the gray mist. Something loomed ahead. Could it possibly be...? A house!

The small white structure looked different from what she remembered, not as large nor the roof as pitched. But this had to be Glinbrendan. She ran to the door and rapped loudly. "Hello? Is anyone home?"

A young woman opened the door, her eyebrows raised in inquiry, a hand to the dark braid lying across her shoulder. Cass racked her memory for the names of Michael's sisters.

"Fiona?" she ventured.

"My name is Katrine."

"Of course, Katrine! I didn't recognize you. Katrine, is Michael here? Is your mother here?"

"Michael?"

Cass's hopes plunged as she saw the restrained curiosity in the woman's eyes. "Michael O'Shea. I was looking for Glinbrendan, for the home of the O'Sheas. I thought..." Her voice failed as she took in the woman's stylish business suit and the room behind her, furnished with contemporary furniture. No hearth for the *Daoine Sidh* here.

"I'm afraid I've never heard of a place round here by that name."

"I know." Cass turned away to hide her gathering tears.

"Would you be wanting a cup of tea before you go? You look like you could use one."

"No, thank you," she managed to say. "I don't hav
time." She walked away, head down, aware of moistur
on her cheeks.

"You'd best come back," the woman called. "There'
a storm brewing."

Storm? Overhead, layers of dull grey clouds closed ir
Rain, perhaps, Cass thought, but no storm. No passio
roiled in those clouds, no charges of excitement to ser
elation singing through her as it had in Michael's storn

She jogged away empty-hearted, feeling the mi:
thicken and merge into a sad quiet drizzle. At last in th
distance she saw the fairy *rath*.

Inside, she walked wearily to the base of a tall cottor
wood, the leaves forming a protective umbrella abov
her. She dropped down, and, resting her forehead on h
knees, let the tears fall.

At a faint sound, she raised her head. Only the stead
patter of rain reached her ears.

Wait. The sound came again. She heard music.
melody, soft and sweet, shifting in and out of a mind
key. The pain in her heart stung bittersweet. How cou
her memories punish her so cruelly? The melodies drifte
around her, coming from nowhere and everywhere, fa
ing and lifting.

"For a wife till death I am willing to take ye..." Tl
words were round and soft.

"Michael?"

*"But, och! I waste my breath, the devil himself can
wake ye..."*

She sprang to her feet. "Michael!"

"'Tis just beginning to rain, so I'll get under cover...
He was here! She could feel it. "Where are you?"

"Come again tomorrow, and be my constant lover.'

"Michael, I will. I'll come every day." She swung round, searching for him. "I believe, Michael. I beeve in you," she cried out. "Please, oh, please—"

"Only love is enough, Cass."

She whirled, her breath stalled in her throat. He stood n the other side of the *rath,* thumbs hooked in the ockets of his tweed work pants, legs slightly apart, just s he'd been that first day.

"Michael…" She could scarcely breathe to whisper his ame. She wanted to run to him, to be in his arms, to ave him hold her forever. But she didn't know how to ad the question in his eyes.

"Whatever are you doing in Ireland, Cass, when you ere so anxious to be gone forever?" His quiet tone beed the lightness of his words.

"I…was concerned about you. I wasn't sure if you'd e able to travel…without me." Uncertainty stayed her, ecked her desire to touch him, to feel the solid strength him against her and know that he was there…there! ot disappeared, not lost. "Oh, Michael…"

Would he turn away from her one last time? Would he away from her forever?

He held her gaze, every question she'd ever seen in his es gone, replaced by a warmth that fanned to sparks. *Tha gaol agam ort,"* he murmured, his eyes full of cerinty now. "I love you, Cass." He slipped his thumbs om his pockets and held out his hands.

Gaol. Love. He'd left her a message of love.

Suddenly, her feet had wings. She flew to him, meetg him halfway across the *rath* where he swept her up, rying his face in the hollow of her neck.

"Cass, *Macushla,* my darling," he crooned softly. He d her, his body solid and strong, more real than anyg she'd ever known. She reached for his kiss, and his

lips closed over hers, igniting desire that slashed throug
her like heat lightning. He sought her with his mouth, h
kiss growing more fierce, more pressing, until his tong
found hers, filling her, tasting her, making her weak.

This storm raged with magnificence. Like the wind, h
driving kisses snatched away her breath. Like the rain, h
hands swept over her, stroking, cherishing, cupping h
breasts, sending passion cascading through her, threa
ening to drown her in a flood of joy. She returned his c
resses, her fingers aching to know him, to be assure
beyond doubt that he'd returned safely, that he stoc
there with her.

She reached for the buttons of his softly textured shir
and he let her slide her hands against his hair-roughene
chest. He watched her watching him, his eyes turning
blue smoke, his look no longer questioning but filled wi
promises, that he was real, that his love knew no bound
that together they would enchant each other beyor
anything she'd ever dreamed.

He kissed her as sweetly and gently as the first kiss
young love, then reached to stroke away a wisp of h
from her cheek, his touch tender and cherishing.

"I love you, Michael," she whispered, pressing agair
his solid body, arching for his lips that gave her fanta
and poetry and belief without end.

"I know." His smile tugged at the corners of his ey
filling them with whimsy.

"Michael, how could you know when all I ever did w
deny you?"

" 'Twas when the sweet old lady on the airplane wo
up and spoke to me." He broke into a full grin.

She could only stare at him in wonder.

"Aye, Cass. 'Twas about midday yesterday, I believ
when you finally stopped being so hardheaded and

your heart see. Gave me a devil of a time getting home, you did. 'Tis no small task being a person where there wasn't one before. You'll have a lot to teach me. That is, if you'll have me.''

"I want you more than anything in life, Michael.''

"My lovely Cass,'' he whispered, covering her mouth with kisses. "I want you as only a man can want his first love. But I am still of the *Daoine Sidh*. Our lovers always wait. Will you wait with me, Cass?''

"Wait? Michael, you're not going away again, are you?'' She grasped the edges of his open shirt.

"Cass, don't you recognize a proposal of marriage?''

"Michael!'' She threw her arms around his neck and buried her face in his shoulder. Drawing back, she placed a finger on his chin. "You have to promise never to disappear.''

"Never,'' Michael murmured. "I never could, Cass, not as long as you love me.''

"So you see, Bren, the story means that we must always believe in the ones we love, *and* in ourselves.'' Cass brushed a shock of curly hair from Brendan's eyes. "Time to sleep, wee one. Grandma Pegeen'll be looking for you tomorrow.''

"May I ride with Grandpa?''

"Of course. He told me there's no better rider in Country Kildare than Brendan O'Shea.''

"Mommy, if I'm extra good, may I sleep over?'' His smile crinkled his deep blue eyes.

So like his father's, Cass thought. For a five-year-old, he was as full of the blarney as his father, too.

"Sure, Pegeen would hear of nothing else.'' From the doorway, Michael smiled proudly at his son. "And when we come for you, I'll have the biggest trophy in the world to show you.''

''Will Seven's Secret win the race?''

''Aye, son.'' Michael kissed the boy, rumpled his hair, then took Cass's hand and drew her after him to their own room.

In the darkness, they crossed to the window to look out at the night. Michael stood behind Cass, sliding his arms around her, resting his cheek against hers and his hands on the small curve of her stomach where a new life was growing.

They gazed at the land outside, tinged in moonlight to the horizon where it sloped into Glinbrendan, the land they'd bought from Michael's boss, Hugh Finnegan. Cass's earnings from her work in Dublin, —''number magic,'' Michael called it—helped make the payments.

Hidden in the far west corner of their property lay the fairy ring, the *rath,* with Michael's training track nearby where he'd trained Seven's Secret.

Michael had raised the thoroughbred for Hugh Finnegan from a colt, had trained him exclusively. He believed in him, and Cass felt sure he would win the race tomorrow.

''Seven for a secret never to be told.'' How well she remembered Michael's words and the seventh secret. She'd taken too long a time to find it out.

Michael nuzzled her, kissing her in the soft hollow behind her ear, down the side of her neck, along her shoulder. She turned to meet his kiss, and his mouth teased her lips, nibbling softly, until she could wait no more. She pulled him nearer, opening to his kiss, to enchantment and fantasy and a passion that swept over them in starlit waves. They clung together, their kisses deepening, until he caught her up and carried her to their bed.

She felt the strong solidness of his body against hers as they flowed together, and she reveled in the joy of the seventh secret. Belief. Trust. Love. The best of the three was the loving.

*   *   *   *   *

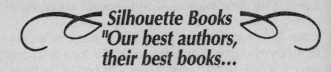

Silhouette Books
"Our best authors,
their best books...

DIANA PALMER
Soldier of Fortune in February

ELIZABETH LOWELL
Dark Fire in February

LINDA LAEL MILLER
Ragged Rainbow in March

JOAN HOHL
California Copper in March

LINDA HOWARD
An Independent Wife in April

HEATHER GRAHAM POZZESSERE
Double Entendre in April

When it comes to passion,
we wrote the book.

SPRING
fancy
'94

**They're sexy, single...
and about to get snagged!**

Passion is in full bloom as love catches
the fancy of three brash bachelors. You won't
want to miss these stories by three of
Silhouette's hottest authors:

**CAIT LONDON
DIXIE BROWNING
PEPPER ADAMS**

Spring fever is in the air this March—
and there's no avoiding it!

Only from

Silhouette®

where passion lives.

SF94

HE'S MORE THAN A MAN,
HE'S ONE OF OUR

Fabulous Fathers

CALEB'S SON
by Laurie Paige

Handsome widower Caleb Remmick had a business to run and a son to raise—alone. Finding help wasn't easy—especially when the only one offering was Eden Sommers. Years ago he'd asked for her hand, but Eden refused to live with his workaholic ways. Now his son, Josh, needed someone, and Eden was the only woman he'd ever trust—and the only woman he'd ever loved....

Look for *Caleb's Son* by Laurie Paige, available in March.

Fall in love with our Fabulous Fathers!

Silhouette
ROMANCE™

FF394

**It's our 1000th
Silhouette Romance
and we're celebrating!**

Join us for a special collection of love stories by the authors you've loved for years, and new favorites you've just discovered.

**It's a celebration just for you,
with wonderful books by
Diana Palmer, Suzanne Carey,
Tracy Sinclair, Marie Ferrarella,
Debbie Macomber, Laurie Paige,
Annette Broadrick, Elizabeth August
and MORE!**

Silhouette Romance...vibrant, fun and emotionally rich! Take another look at us!

As part of the celebration, readers can receive a FREE gift AND enter our exciting sweepstakes to win a grand prize of $1000! Look for more details in all March Silhouette series titles.

**You'll fall in love all over again
with Silhouette Romance!**

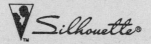

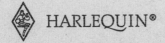